FROM REVIEWS OF ~~GUN~~
BY JOAN ~~BURBICK~~

"A brilliant and insightful reading of America's gun culture, rooted in the history of social violence, which illuminates the conflict between 'gun rights' and civil rights in American Democracy."
— RICHARD SLOTKIN, historian and novelist,
Gunfighter Nation: Myth of the Frontier
in Twentieth Century America

"*Gun Show Nation* provides an indispensable ethnographic guide to America's obsession with guns. Anyone interested in understanding the future of gun control and the remarkable resiliency of gun rights in American culture will need to grapple with Burbick's richly nuanced study of gun shows."
— SAUL CORNELL, historian, *A Well-Regulated Militia:*
The Founding Fathers and the Origins of Gun Control in America

"Burbick serves up a delectable slice of Americana."
— *Atlantic Journal-Constitution*

"[Burbick] is capable of showing us both the glitter and the glamour of the rodeo subculture, and at the same time, some of its deepest contradictions."
—*Los Angeles Times*

"This book tells a story about The West that has not been told before. And it tells it with clarity, humor, faith, skepticism, and a guarded kind of love (which is the best kind of love.) Rodeo Queens are just as important to the idea of The West as Indian chiefs and gunfighters, but more important as their story has not been told."
— SHERMAN ALEXIE, novelist and poet,
The Absolutely True Diary of a Part-Time Indian

STRIPLAND

REDBAT BOOKS
PACIFIC NORTHWEST WRITERS SERIES

JOAN BURBICK

STRIPLAND

a novel

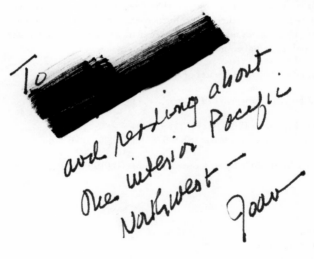

To ~~_____~~
and petting about
the interior Pacific
Northwest —
Joan

redbat
books

redbat books
2019

Printed in the United States of America

First Edition: June 4, 2019

Trade Paperback ISBN 978-1-946970-94-7
Hardcover with Dust Jacket ISBN 978-1-946970-88-6

Library of Congress Control Number: 2019941179

Published by
redbat books
La Grande, OR 97850
www.redbatbooks.com

Text set in Mrs Eaves

Cover Art:
Based on original photograph of Lewiston, Idaho by Jenny Ennvy

Cover Design & Book Layout:
Kristin Summers, redbat design | www.redbatdesign.com

ALSO BY JOAN BURBICK

*Thoreau's Alternative History: Changing Perspectives
on Nature, Culture and Language*

*Healing the Republic: The Language of Health and the Culture
of Nationalism in Nineteenth-Century America*

Rodeo Queens and the American Dream

Gun Show Nation: Gun Culture and American Democracy

*Beyond Imagined Uniqueness:
Nationalisms in Contemporary Perspectives (edited)*

For Patti, Clifford and VE

TABLE OF CONTENTS

PART ONE

MAN WITH THE ROPE

:: ONE ::

It tilted. The sidewalk refused to stay level, the rushing traffic oblivious to his walking and the thick rope attached at his waist, dragging on the concrete. A long trudge to visit the doll of corn-husks with dirty black eyes. Two more miles to Dave's Pawn Shop at the top of the hill. He had come to believe she was his earth angel, keeping the world upright as it hovered within its magneto-sphere, soothing the waves that tumble and tremble, threatening to reverse or disperse, letting solar winds sweep him away into the cold vacuum of space. Encrusted with pebbles, dirt, and cigarette butts, the thick rope anchored him in case the worst happened, which could at any moment though everyone racing past in their fixed stare knew nothing.

Years ago, when he could still read, he spent seven Wednesday nights in a row at the city library listening to a retired astron-omer show slides of cosmic catastrophes, exploding stars, nu-clear storms, and drifting galaxies that devoured planets where he imagined small children, inside homes watching television. The astro-image of a fluctuating magnetic field dancing over the north and south poles crumpled his insides. One slide shown for a few seconds changed him forever in the small arc of his life, now knowing nothing rested, merely hovered, waiting for the cat-aclysm that no one could see because the field was invisible, made up of waves that only scientists with their strange equipment could envision. His task was simply to stay walking with his rope caress-ing the gritty concrete.

Only the corn doll in her complete stillness knew how to keep the earth steady. What did astronomers really know? They only measured what was happening. The doll had no machines. She stood in her glass case staring, unblinking, certain. Only she kept the lines from tumbling into a mass of tangled skeins, strangling the earth. Only she knew what would happen.

He had seen the doll once before when his sister picked him up from the little blue house near McDonald's where he lived with Henry who talked about sandwiches. She had driven him slow-ly up the steep hill along 21st Street until it changed into Thain Avenue near the wide ravine that stretched beyond his eyes. He remembered because in the car she talked about how beds were good. He knew beds were good, but they were not necessary, not since he had walked away from the blue house with its bed because the corn doll was calling him.

She would make everything stop trembling.

There was a friend who could have helped him navigate the magnetosphere, but another man shot him. The corn doll prob-ably knew why. If he kept walking the steep sidewalk, she might even erase the face of the man who killed his friend. She could do anything. His shoulders aching from the effort to drag the rope, he strayed far from the blue house. The bed was not for him. Not anymore.

For weeks, the interior of the pawnshop had appeared in the night no matter where he slept, tossing in a torn sleeping bag, hiding in a recycled cardboard box, or resting in a beautiful red plastic sphere. The doll could have chosen somewhere else to live, somewhere closer like the steep concrete building with the fish sign or the large aluminum shed with the long white dagger cross pointing to heaven and earth. People went in and out free-ly, singing. He could hear them singing from the blue house. He didn't know why she chose the pawnshop at the top of the hill. 2.4 miles away.

He tried to tell his sister and Henry before he left. *Don't talk like that*, they said. *Don't talk. Be quiet. Life will get better. Believe me. Let's go eat sandwiches. Subway sandwiches. Let's go to the river and look at the water and how the light plays on the surface* as if the river would stop the shaking of the magnetosphere.

The mission was clear. Life was crystal as Henry liked to say. Crystal clear. Crystal like the pawnshop on the first visit where he went with his sister to *get some fresh air.*

Bent, dented aluminum-framed windows glinted from the square corner, their siding stained with mud and dog pee. The man inside the crumbling store had smiled that crooked mouth-grin and said nothing when he came in, only looked down for a brief second and nodded. Was he talking to himself? The owner tried not to look at the thick rope that was hard to pull past the heavy glass door, dragging in scraps of paper, and instead stood straight behind the case and let him come close to the doll that seemed to know he was coming. There was nothing else in the store for him.

"Hey look," his sister said, "eight *Pretty Woman*," her finger sliding down a tall stack of used DVDs.

The owner wore a brown flannel shirt in shades of sand and dark blood and whispered if he wanted to see the doll up close. The store was nearly empty, and the keeper had decided on impulse to talk to the man with the rope. He reached inside the case and brought the corn doll out, its face, two black seeds in a sphere like the earth that spins in total faith.

With his face almost touching the doll's head, the man with the rope felt the same jolt as on that evening at the library sitting in back watching slides whirl past with galaxies beyond beauty in their cold luminescence, eviscerating his equilibrium.

Her eyes had everything inside, waiting to transform into life forms that blinked at the sun before death. They told the man with the rope how light would only last so long, how day would soon become night, how the rope was good no matter how covered in dirt because it would help him stay on the sidewalk while everything else would rush past, soaring into the void. Her words were clear and certain.

He thanked the owner who returned the doll to its case ever so gently as if lifting a leaf dried and withered. The owner announced that he would never sell the doll. It was essential to lock her up because other customers might come in at any moment and bend over the cases of guns, tired musical instruments, banged trombones and mouthed-dirty harmonicas, and then edge toward her case and want to touch the seed-eyes.

Weeks ago, the doll had spoken to him, but he didn't understand the words. Maybe someday he would. He asked the man with the rope if he knew what they meant. He nodded yes, but in this one brief exchange of words he said he could not tell the keeper of the doll. No word spoken twice would last. The owner would have to wait. The doll would talk again when she was ready. The owner should prepare.

After that day, the doll's keeper looked with exquisite tenderness at the front door waiting for the man with the rope to return, and after a few months he began to stare at the door when the doll started to talk, and when she would not stop talking, making his mind spin and spurt, he wanted to burn the doll or bury it behind the shed, but he knew he had no choice, other than to wait for the man with the rope to walk back through the door. He sat behind the counter, his eyes locked until his fury made him hate his store and everything in it, the aging men looking for something they would never find and pretending it was a discarded tool or a scratched handgun, a pile of unread *Popular Mechanics*, the cracked cups and plates remaindered after death, the thin film of filth covering everything except for what he kept in the back vaults that the doll kept talking about, her words ticking off a complete inventory.

:: TWO ::

When he left Green Star Avenue and the blue house, Henry warned him. "Someone will hurt you," his roommate shouted down the street.

Henry had packed him tuna on white, scolding the bread and the pickles with a hand flip into the dirty brown backpack, hot vinegar words smeared on the sandwich.

"That's why I have my rope," he yelled back.

"Your stupid rope. I hate your rope. I hope you lose it." Henry slammed the front door.

Outside screaming was bad for neighbor ears, listening at the window before they called the police. That lady in the yellow house with the blood roses like her mouth, her front lawn covered in blood, would peek and call. *Lady Peek and Call* he muttered, heading to 21ˢᵗ and McDonald's.

Two blocks south on Green Star then left on 7ᵗʰ Avenue due east where he knew the hills rose up miles away, scabby patches crisscrossed with other roads in the distance, too vague to remember the long years spent journeying to a job he no longer could recall. Then 7ᵗʰ over to 21ˢᵗ.

Henry said that streets were more important than avenues. Henry lied all the time. He would never lose his rope because the rope was tied fast around his waist with a knot he learned in Boy Scouts, two half-hitches go around two and a half times more. A pipe hitch. What Mr. Bowman called a death grip. The rope would have to lose him. And that would never happen because it was attached to him and the sidewalk as he walked from Green Star to 21st, his feet gripping the firm concrete path, far away from moving mouths bickering about sandwiches.

Once he had watched as men poured thick muddy globs into delicate grids of string and carefully smoothed the shifting blobs to the edges and twisted trowels into curves until a surface appeared out of muck, their hands caking with beige chunks that split and flaked onto their arms. He sat on the rise above the men and watched the sidewalk grow into a line to the top of the hill. Over the summer, a dirty path at the side of the busy road changed into a walkway giving him, without the curbs, intervening cross streets, odd interruptions, a flue, a storm drain, poorly placed electrical boxes and pumps, more than two miles of concrete walk to find the corn doll. Today his efforts to cross 21st at 7th exhausted him, and he barely made it back to the blue house before collapsing on the front room couch with no springs.

"Did you eat your sandwich?" Henry grabbed his backpack, unzipped the top, then tossed it on the floor. "It's still there."

His eyes adjusting to the dark room, the man with the rope scrunched his shoulders against the back padding of the sofa. He wanted to crawl inside. Jerry and Austin sat on the floor eating tiny sausages out of a tin. Jerry didn't look at the man with the rope. He didn't like to look at people because his heart was big, too big for his eyes. His greasy flak jacket had spoons and cups dangling from hooks, a kitchen in motion. Old cellphones stuck out of his left pocket. The man with the rope looked at Jerry but didn't look at Austin. He didn't want to talk with Austin. Skinny eyes with a hawk mouth, Austin told him stories he didn't believe, and said only one book had all the stories ever needed.

The man with the rope hated what Henry called visitors, the stream of men drifting into the living room for a break, a shower, then a disappearance. They brought trouble and shouldn't be there. His sister, Sunday, said so and threatened to tell the authorities. The police called them bums or skells. *Lady Peek and Call* probably had a list with full descriptions, just in case her car disappeared. Her list: drug and disease carriers, criminals-in-waiting, released criminals, lost men in need of found prisons. Zero degree of tolerance. Safety first.

Jerry had no answers to anything the man with the rope asked, and Austin had every answer ever needed; Jerry had dead cellphones and Austin had the book.

"You better wash that rope," laughed Austin.

"Leave him," cut in Jerry, wiping out the tin can and sticking it into his pants pocket.

The man with the rope wanted to speak bad words into Austin's face. He wanted to ask him what Jesus was doing for those three days after he was crucified and buried. Those three days he could have been somewhere else besides hell. He might have stayed in his tomb or wandered back into Jerusalem or maybe even consulted with the corn doll. She might have told him stories for three days. What could Satan have told him for three days or those dead ones writhing in pain that he didn't know already? Satan had hung out around Jesus plenty when he was alive, those forty days and nights in the wilderness, a trip to the holy city and the high mountain. Jesus knew the tempter in and out. Why go back to hell and visit the devil? Why not tell us the truth? Three days in hell didn't make sense. Three days checking the magnetosphere made more sense. Finding out how many more days before the end of earth days, that made the most sense. Jesus should have told us how many more days before earth vanished.

He walked into the back room curling the rope around his waist and closed the door. The room smelled of rose and pine needles. His sister Sunday had left a big bowl that he nibbled on even though she said not to eat it. It was only for a smell to make him feel better. He sat down on his bed and wondered what Venus smelled like with its rolling waves of carbon dioxide and clouds of sulfuric acid because all the hydrogen had been swept away by a cosmic wind, no internal magnetic sphere, no plate tectonics like earth, no magnetosphere to protect the planet from fury. Maybe Venus smelled like hell, icky smells like gasoline and paint. Smell Hell. He walked over to the bowl and cupped his hands inside, lifting the dried petals and sharp needles to his nose. They smelled of Sunday's house by the river. The sadness made him spill the smell on the floor, pull the rope in tight and find his way back to bed. He had to find his way back to sleep. Set the clock for three am. Start again to find the corn doll.

Before sunrise, he would try to get to the Comfort Inn with his uneaten sandwich. He must try again. The waves of cars, pick-up trucks, bicycles, and motorcycles on 21st stopped him yesterday and would not let him pass, like when the Red Sea parted that Austin kept talking about as if it happened yesterday. Last night, Jerry had made him a map with red-yellow-green blinking eyes.

In early morning, he would try again to walk uphill recalculated two point four miles on the east side still under the cover of darkness but after the night sirens and boys up to no good.

:: THREE ::

The W in the sky revolved overhead as he strained his neck to read the other letters. Dimmed by the reflected neon lights lining 21st, the night was a black puddle with only a handful of stars. On the next block, a sliced sun in waves of deep yellow and orange illuminated the gateway to the Comfort Inn. A narrow row of at-attention shrubs promenaded around the spotless beige building. He was walking uphill to 8th Avenue when the drunken buzz of the streetlight made him think of insects that crawled on the screen porch when he was little. He would pop the screen with his thumb and index finger and send them flying. Some had tiny mouths and rubbed their filaments together. Others had curved claws digging into the hatches of the screen. They wanted inside.

He went over to the streetlight, a long, shiny-smooth aluminum post, and placed his right ear on the surface. The buzz sounded like a frantic world of shrill shouts and cries over a bass droning. The cool dark of the night with its crystalline W topped the buzz, connecting him to a magnetic line. The post might grab a single current and hurl it into the metallic ocean inside the earth. These poles snaking the sidewalk of 21st Street could be conduits that gathered and propelled the earth's magnetic field through Lewiston to the corn doll's home.

He pulled the street map Jerry had made and compared the markings with the deserted four-lane highway and its empty box stores and fast food restaurants. *Stripland* is what Jerry called it.

"There is nothing in *Stripland*," Jerry cautioned him before he left.

Stripland was built to make us forget where we came from and where we were going. Jerry believed in cutting across fields and sleeping under his tarp at the edge of ravines. Smell the soil.

"No one walks on 21st. Not even the locals. It is only for machines, not you or me." They built that sidewalk to fool the people. Stupefy. Make everyone forget that the street was for mowing down walkers.

"Cross on green," Henry added when the two men had crawled out of their sleeping bags. The man with the rope had tried to leave the blue house without notice, but he caught a strap of his backpack in the door jamb in the front hallway as he left.

"Don't tell Sunday," he whispered in the dark before he closed the door gently pulling his rope out of the way of the hinge snap.

The night was best for garbage, sticky pizza scraps, hash browns, and fish sticks, no big bags of oranges at Albertsons like Henry said. In the morning, he tried to walk across the street on green so people would not yell at him. Across from McDonald's, a young girl waved when he stepped into the rush of cars, squeezing his fingers. She knew red and green. He tried to cross the roar, but the noise made his head hurt. She waved again and started to step away from the yellow arches when a woman screamed and tugged her back. He wanted to help the girl, but 21st was charging at him, big trucks skidding and cars veering. Was the girl trying to escape *Stripland*? He saw a young woman with long blond hair drive past combing her hair as if there was nothing wrong with the stream of belch and fumes.

After that, only night. Stay away from people going fast on a conveyor belt like the machine he saw on TV, two circles connected with precise arcs by a mathematical formula to keep everything going around and never going anywhere.

He was going somewhere.

Throwing his rope over his shoulder, he pledged to walk faster until a scraping sound at the back of a parking lot with spaces for almost a hundred cars made him flinch. There weren't supposed to be people in *Stripland* past midnight.

The sound continued, a dull, rasping noise, not like the humming of the power generator at the back of the grocery store. Maybe someone was trying to dig a tunnel under *Stripland*. Jerry would admire that plan. He could bypass the gawking drivers and crawl under the highway.

Jerry had valuable information. At the blue house, he had said that cougars might still roam the ravine at the top of 21st and had handed the man with the rope a map scribbled on the back of a Subway menu with red stars for possible sightings. "Maybe you'll run into one of those cougars."

"Don't listen." Henry had shouted back. "Those cougars are long gone. You just come home soon. I don't want your sister hounding me." He had gone into his bedroom and come back with a black mobile phone. "Only text left. Type in *a* and push send. I'm the only one you can send a message. Type in *a* if there is a problem. Okay?"

"I'm not stupid," the man with the rope had snapped, slipping the small black phone that he would never use into his backpack.

Maybe he could sell it, he thought, fingering the phone in his pocket as he listened to the scraping sound. It was coming from the empty parking lot in front of Subway.

When he got close, the man with the rope could see that the empty store was glowing from the dimmed overhead ceiling lights. The stainless table behind the counter with its vinyl shield gleamed like a surgical surface waiting for its next patient. The large poster menus proudly displayed columns of thick layers of meat covered in slices of onions and cheese. The bread racks looked strange empty since he could smell the herbs and cheese. Where do they put the bread at night, he wondered? He used to drive to this store in his work life. Fast park. Brisk walk inside. Order to the smiling face. Watch your flattened sub enter on the straight conveyor belt to toast inside the oven, a magical moment. The first taste of tender chicken blanketed in shreds of lettuce.

He stared at the sign. The *SUB* went one way with the *S* pointing north; the *WAY* went in the opposite direction, the *Y* pointing south. That was bad. The sign couldn't make up its mind. That was why it was two different colors, white and yellow, not like the Comfort Inn, one circle, with beautiful curves, all four colors inside. No confusion about where to go. Come right in and sleep.

Pressing his face against the cool glass, he rested his fingers above his head. The fluorescent light started to make him feel wide awake. He worried if he was too wide awake. Too many ultra-violet rays would cause prickly pain to creep down his arms and into his face. The tingles in his jaw and cheeks would turn into shouts, then daggers.

The return of the scraping noise made him step back from the window. Was someone dragging a metal bar across the concrete? He'd heard about the night boys from Henry. *Don't let them get my phone.* They would take everything and leave you naked but unhurt, if they were in a good mood. The night boys were tricky. Henry said they could appear in more than one place at once. They never wandered alone, always in clumps of three or four and always at night. The man with the rope had never seen them. He had to decide quickly what to do. The sign was no help. Maybe he should go back to the streetlight.

At the side of the Subway, the lid of a dull blue dumpster was open. Maybe someone was looking for throws.

Glancing back inside, he saw a slim man with glasses and a grooved face walk out of a green shadow. He propped a shovel against the rear wall and came to the front door. The man with the rope felt safe. He could see in, but the man with the shovel could not see out. The skinny man looked worried, cocking his head to hear outside. The two men were pushing middle-age. One with thinning black hair in stiff clumps at the top of his head, the other with no hair and a thick body, a thick neck, and a thick rope twisted around a baggy left pants leg.

"Who's there," the skinny man said.

The man with the rope stepped back further into darkness. He didn't want any trouble. It was the scraping sound that had caused the trouble.

"I know someone is out there," he said with a gentle voice. "Do you want food?"

The man with the rope had heard about people like him. People with food they gave away if you came by at night before closing. But closing was hours ago, and only this worried man with anxious eyes was left in the store. Maybe he was taking food that was not his. Maybe he had used the shovel to force his way through the back door. Why was he trying to get the man with the rope to answer? Did he really have food? Did he want to be his friend? Was he a thief in the night?

"Don't run away." The thin man opened the front door and stuck his head out. "My name is Al. Al Zhang."

:: FOUR ::

The man with the rope folded his empty packet of Sun Chips and stuck it in his backpack. He wanted to thank his new friend, Al, but he didn't know how. They sat across a small metal table in the back room, cluttered with boxes and cleaning supplies. On the wall, a large poster of a couple walking on the beach and holding hands was partly ripped. He wanted to ask Al for some scotch tape. He wanted to fix the poster.

"I have apples." Al pointed to the large refrigerator behind more boxes.

Al liked coming to the restaurant late at night when no one was around to bother him. He was working on a math problem he carried in his head. He had carried it in his head since he was 19 years old, and he was getting close to finishing it. Al told him how he lost the ability to teach math when a young student walked into the main office at his university many miles away to the south and shot his office mate then turned the gun on himself. The blood splattered over his textbook and exam papers, dripping onto his Impetus Jell Pen. The blue covers were speckled with red. "No more teaching," he said, rooting around for another Sun Chips in one of the half-opened boxes. He wasn't afraid, he explained to the man with the rope who sat and listened wondering if this new friend would be someone he could tell about the magnetosphere.

"No more teachers talking. No more talking. Period. Just listen. Like you. A good listener. Do you know, I like my job?

Everyone comes in and wants something different." He paused before continuing. "I once tried to calculate the variations when you list the size and type of bread, the cheeses, vegetables, sauces and meats, maybe two million variations, depending where in the country. Some places don't like tuna or black forest ham. You have to calculate for chance."

"Chance," the man with the rope repeated. He remembered how he would always order the same thing. Never any variation.

"You have to leave soon," Al said glancing at his watch. "Where will you go?"

"Up," the man with the rope pointed to 21st.

"There's nothing up there but more of the same."

Al studied the man with the rope, his eyes resting on his dirty trousers and the stained rope, stuck with burrs and bits of gravel.

"One night," he said abruptly as if he didn't want the words to come out of his mouth. "Sleep in my car until lunch."

"What time is lunch?"

"It's already after four. People start showing around seven. You could have maybe five or six hours. It's the old Volvo parked in the back under the trees beside the dumpster."

Al opened the back door of the storage room and gestured to the dirty white car tucked into the back parking lot, next to a grove of trees. "See. Private."

The man with the rope stood behind him and curled his head.

"What time is lunch?" the man repeated.

"11 or 12. What does it matter? Are you going somewhere important?"

The man with the rope placed his finger on his lips, the universal sign of silence.

"A secret? I get it."

"I don't need sleep." He drew his rope closer to his feet.

He didn't know if he could trust his new friend. Al was helpful. Helpful was dangerous. Helpful people wanted something, like your cellphone or your wallet. He even met a helpful person who wanted his soul.

But he wanted Al to talk about chance. It didn't matter if he always ordered oven-roasted chicken breast on 9-grain honey oat with lettuce, tomato, and light mayo. Like it didn't matter if banana peppers looked like slugs. Anyway, he tried not to see them when he stood in line ordering. Sometimes that was impossible because people who like banana peppers shouted out banana peppers and pointed to the tray behind the vinyl shield. But in the magnetic field chance mattered.

"The back seat slants. There's a soft blanket in a Safeway shopping bag." Al stepped outside the back door.

"Chance?" The man with the rope insisted, imagining arrhythmic solar flares, substorms and broken radiation belts assaulting the earth.

Frustrated, Al came back inside and closed the door.

"Yes, chance. One man wanted cookies crumbled and put on his sandwich, but his wife objected, and I had to crumble them in secret and sprinkle them on right before I folded the paper tight. Worse, you might have someone at any time walk in with something they want to put on their sandwich like mini marshmallows or seasoning from home. You're not supposed to take these things and put them on the sandwich, but they would unwrap what you had carefully wrapped and lace the sandwich. Maybe even marijuana buds. Who knows? That's the problem. You don't know."

The man with the rope listened, cocking his head through the further variations of extra cheese, yogurt, sriracha sauce, Al, granola, M&M'S, and sprinkles. It was clear that the list consisted of hundreds of separate items, maybe thousands. How could there be so many variations?

"40 million or more. Believe me. Who's to tell when you include chance, unless you have some other grid to determine home-manufactured or privately-purchased variations eaten in the store. How would you count a package of leftover oyster crackers that a customer found in her purse and on impulse spilled over her sandwich for more crunch? If they take the sandwich out of the store, I guess it wouldn't count. No good parameters."

Al should make the customers empty their pockets and leave their backpacks and handbags behind the counter. Before they picked up their sandwich, they must show both sides of their hands. No tricks. When they ate, they would be monitored for unnecessary gestures. Only the items on the menu would be allowed. On second thought, he knew it wouldn't work. The customers would take their food outside and sit in their parked cars or on the curb in front of the Subway and munch on whatever they had brought from their refrigerators or kitchen drawers to put on their sandwiches: pretzels, walnuts, salty licorice, popcorn, bananas, wads of butter, PEZ from the Batman dispensers, and chewed gum. There was no way to stop them just as there was no way to stop the magnetosphere from folding and flipping, its current whipping above and around earth.

Interrupting, the man with the rope asked Al if he could consult with him about something very important, more important than anything in the world, even food or water.

Al nodded.

"Do you know about the magnetosphere?"

:: FIVE ::

A sweating plastic bottle of Dawn Pot and Pan Detergent sat
in the middle of the folding table, the bright blue liquid reaching
above the thick label with its guarantee of long-lasting suds and
hot water savings. In the chlorine-soaked storage room, the tall
bottle glowed from the light of the dangling fluorescent tubes.

"It takes time to find the right solution."

Sitting across from the man with the rope, Al calmly described his daily routine at Subway, trying to avoid any more talk
about the magnetosphere, gibberish that made his head ache.
He had never heard of an ESA cluster or NASA's THEMIS and
doubted if the man with the rope understood magnetic flips and
reversals or a single equation of magnetohydrodynamics, even
though he insisted he had the latest data to predict events up to
a certain variable. As the vagrant talked in crescendo about the
popping and drifting of magnetic poles, Al worried that he had
made a mistake feeding him and offering him his car. Obsessions made Al squirm and sweat. And he didn't like the way the
rope was curled tightly around the man's left leg, squeezing his
thigh as he described the pattern of pole reversals every 200,000
to 300,000 years.

Cleaning might help. It certainly helped Al calm down when
he remembered the tangy smell of blood splattered across his blue
exam covers. What good would fixating on the magnetosphere
do if anyone could walk into your office at any time and shoot
themselves in the head? Scrubbing soothed. Al could see how the

homeless man needed a daily practice to counteract his anxiety. A sponge was what he needed.

"Cleaning is mathematical," Al asserted in a cheerful voice. "Careful steps with wild leaps like the day I used baking soda on the trashcan. I had tried everything. Methodical. Then in a flash it came to me."

The man with the rope kept staring at the Dawn detergent. "Why is it blue?" he asked.

"Blue? I don't know. The sky?"

"Maybe the sky," the man paused, examining the bottle. "The blue looks sick. How could it get in the bottle?"

"It's not really sky, only chemicals in water." He wondered if the man with the rope could read. Maybe he couldn't even think, his brain addled with drugs or booze. Did he really think the sky was in the bottle? He didn't look dangerous. He wanted to ask about the rope. Instead, he got up and walked over to the stacked cleaning supplies against the wall and pointed to the correct product for each activity on the Night Shift Checklist.

"Soup areas are not the same as the bread cabinet. Tables have stubborn spots because people can be dirty and their children worse. Bubble gum is a nightmare. Sanitizing takes vigilance."

Checklist in hand, the man with the rope followed Al around the storage area. "**TEAMWORK IS THE GOAL**" was printed in bold, capital letters across the top. Underneath words in plain type battled with words in bold while words in italics crashed into words underlined. The capital letters screamed. The bold demanded, the italics pleaded, and the underlined threatened. A cacophony hurting his eyes. Cautiously examining both sides of the checklist, he held it up to the ceiling light and realized the letters made no sense. He brought the list up to his face.

"Why 13?" he asked.

"It's not the ten commandments," explained Al, taking the sheet back. "There are 13 items that must be completed every night."

Disappointed with the answer, he shrugged his shoulders and walked around the storage room in a counterclockwise direction, looking at each cleaning product perched on the metal cabinets. He stopped at the Comet Cleanser bottle, taking it from the shelf and pointing it at a spot on the wall. "Numbers are better than letters," he said, starting to twist the top of the spray bottle.

"Careful with that," Al cautioned. "That has bleach, man's best friend in the battle against bacteria and viruses."

Gently, he took the cleaner from him, placing it back on the shelf.

"Is it from a comet?" the man with the rope asked, his hands trembling.

Al almost laughed but instead reassured him in a voice he once heard his mother use. He didn't know why it was named Comet. Maybe it had to do with power, a cosmic force coming to earth and wiping out the bad germs.

"I know about comets," the man with the rope murmured as he walked to the Comet and peered at its label before backing away. "I won't touch it."

"Why don't you rest?" Al asked softly. "My car is safe. You can sleep."

Why did Al repeat the same things as his sister? They both wanted him to sleep as if sleep would make him like before when he lived without his rope. Would sleep erase what he saw on the man's face? Would it stop the earth from trembling? Maybe they wanted to steal his rope when he was asleep. Sleep was dangerous, naps best with one eye open.

"Comets can affect the magnetosphere," he finally asserted, ignoring Al's suggestion.

Al stared at the spray bottle back on the metal shelf and cocked his head as if hearing the man with the rope for the first time.

"Magnetosphere?" asked Al, secretly hoping to divert his attention. Feign ignorance. Change the conversation. Appear detached.

"The solar winds." The man with the rope pointed to the ceiling. "They are out there beyond our magnetosphere waiting to rip us apart like the comets that fall from the Oort Cloud to their death in the sky. The comets are trying to reach us."

The sadness in the man with the rope's voice startled Al.

"It's okay," he said quickly, surprised at his own concern. "I don't know your name." Who was this homeless person who had drifted into the store after hours looking for leftovers? Then he remembered the man hadn't asked for anything. "Don't you want to sleep?"

"Will you steal my rope?"

"No, I don't want your rope."

The early morning light was starting to gather and the man with the rope understood he had limited time left. "Okay."

"Good," muttered Al, leading the man out the back door to his dirty, white car.

"It's not much, but look, the back is pulled down. There are three pillows and another blanket in the black plastic bag. Don't worry. I'll keep an eye out if anyone gets close to the car."

"I have this," the man with the rope said, pulling out of his pocket a handful of change. He handed Al a shiny quarter. "I found this one today."

Polished to a glitter, the quarter looked like any other, except for the shine.

Al tried to give it back. "I don't need payment. Anytime. Anytime, you come here, there is always food and this car." He tried to return the coin.

"No," he said sharply. "Too dangerous for me."

Arguing about money was not good. He knew he would never come back. He would leave as soon as dark came again. He could hear traffic on 21st starting to increase, pickups accelerating to charge up the steep incline. If he stayed a second night, Al would start whispering friendly words to give him courage like at the hospital daycare. Al meant well like the nurses. None of them knew about the corn doll and how he had to walk two more miles to visit her. They lived in the traffic and the square buildings by the highways and had forgotten why they lived on the planet.

Before he fell asleep, he remembered the night he saw a comet fall in the sky, its beautiful tail, a pencil-thin white fading to black.

:: SIX ::

Night lights from Mount Zion Baptist illuminated the water drainage where he hastily set up shelter on a patch of dirt above the filthy creek cutting through the weedy ditch below the parking lot. Having hidden for three blocks past the Comfort Inn, he had made it to the 11th Avenue intersection with 21st and walked toward the tall, thin cross on the church's front entrance. Neat vinyl-sided houses with tricycles in the backyards surrounded the worship hall, except for the slice of wetlands that dipped just enough to protect the lean-to from the vigilante-eyes of the neighbors. The man with the rope knew he would have to fold up the tarp before dawn. He would have to work quickly with Dog Star rising above the horizon. Light came too early in August. Not enough time to nap because a girl had stumbled into his camp when the sky turned inky dark with some story about how her mother was so lonely that she drank throughout the day, vodka with milk for breakfast, vodka with orange juice for lunch, vodka with ginger ale for dinner. How her mother stayed inside the house, and how her father never came home, but she did both.

The girl's delicate face with its fragile chin and whispering mouth took him aback. For the first hour he listened intently as her floating words filled up the small enclosure, making his heart quiver. She acted as if he was there simply to listen. Her stone, green eyes within an outer ring of high-tension black

scrutinized his face, his clothes, his rope. Sitting in a yoga position two feet away, the girl barely moved her lips. Her eyes were
too big for her face. After two hours, she made his nerves sick.
He could not tell what she wanted. He knew that he could never
tell what anyone was thinking. He used to think he could; now
he knew better. No one lets you in. Not in there. Not inside. He
could not tell what she was thinking, but she wanted inside his
thoughts. Why? He had to protect himself from this fourteen-
year-old who murmured like a hypnotist. Why had she walked
into his makeshift camp as if she was expected? No fear. Not
like the other girls who walked across the street to avoid even
coming close.

They had stayed awake most of the night, huddled in the lean-
to he had made from the tarp he took at the Subway storage room.
The bright blue plastic edge flapped in the wind, snapping in
anger. The entire time, she hadn't asked any questions, but he
sensed she was stalling, pacifying him like his social worker, before she pried information out of him. Her stories were covers,
diversions before she struck.

He thought his own diversion: Describe the parallel computers at the Pittsburgh Supercomputing Center and the Los Alamos
National Laboratory that chart in 3D numerical simulation the
earth's geomagnetic core. Did she know about teraflop, a trillion
calculations per second? If she knew about the supercomputers,
it might stop her whispering. He might have to interrupt her and
insist that she listen.

"What is it?" she asked, sliding her fingers across the end of
the rope that stuck outside the lean-to.

He didn't answer. He never did. And he was disappointed that
she finally asked him a question he would never answer. Maybe
she was not a threat. Maybe she was stuck in a time loop with her
mother who drank vodka from morning until night.

The girl bent down and sniffed the rope.

He jerked back into the lean-to. Her brown, curling hair that draped gracefully around her heart face with its perfect bangs were clean and combed. She couldn't be a runaway. He saw those girls at the edge of Main Street with their greasy hair and drooped mouths, their words spilling because they had no strength to keep them inside. Those weary girls shifted back and forth on their dirty sneakers waiting for the same thing he was waiting for. She must be a mirage or what Helen at the Sunrise Center called a hallucination. The mind could wander, she had cautioned him. He liked the word, *hallucination*. It sounded like *hallelujah*, and the church cross on the white façade had probably summoned her to bother him in his sleep.

"Do you wash it?" she asked.

He hoped she was a dream and he could wake up and she would be gone.

"I could help," she suggested, picking up the end of the rope and brushing off a few leaf specks.

Slowly, she began to dig out the burrs with her fingernails, placing them in a neat pile next to her shoes.

"You are lying," he said, pulling the rope gradually toward his waist, wrapping it around his right wrist.

"About what?"

"Too clean. Too clean."

"Me? Of course, I am clean. I wash my hair every night before I go to bed."

He slid away into the back of the lean-to.

"You have to listen to me." She reached toward his rope and started picking out stubborn debris. "Do you see these seeds?" She gathered a dozen in her palm from the end of his rope. "You could plant these seeds."

She forbade him to look away or cover his ears. For the last two weeks she had climbed out of her bedroom window and slept on the floor of the dance studio where she took ballet lessons every

Monday, Wednesday, and Friday after school. Her ballet teacher, Mrs. Holland, let her sleep in the studio on the mat. She even has a pile of blankets and pillows there. She loved the dance studio. The floor-to-ceiling mirrors shone at night. Sometimes, in the middle of the night, she would *cabriole,* leaping and jumping ready to burst. She multiplied in the mirrors. "You should come there and sleep, not in this dirty, old lean-to. There is a bathroom with a shower. I clean the studio after school on Tuesdays and Thursdays and my parents don't know anything about it. So there. Don't look at me with that long face. I know what you're up to."

How could she know about the corn doll? Maybe she was an emissary, or a secret agent sent to assist his mission. More probably she was sent by his sister, Sunday, or Henry, or Judge Fender. She might be an undercover cop.

"*Pas de Ciseaux*. Have you ever seen it? Stretch up and out, tall, tall. Right shoulder down."

She crawled out of the tarp, stood tall and reached towards the sky with her right arm, running for two seconds and then letting her legs fly apart in a leap of such beauty he wanted to cry out.

"You see I am not lying. That takes practice. Come tonight."

He didn't want to follow her to the studio. He didn't want to follow her anywhere even when she left at dawn and looked at him for a long time before she turned her back and skipped up the hill in front of the church.

The dance studio was between Cash 2 Go and Spring Leaf Financial Services behind 16th Avenue, five blocks away. She had made him a map on a torn piece of notepaper and tucked it in his shirt pocket.

Her face stayed with him after she left. Those stone-green eyes. She couldn't know where he was going. She knew nothing about him. No way she could know about the corn doll. Words aren't about what's inside. She is lying. She is not real.

:: SEVEN ::

Vigilantes had thrown trash at his camp and called the police. He had stayed too long in the lean-to, listening to the girl and worrying whether she was a spy. What did she know and when did she know it? In the distance sirens whirled, threatening his safe exit. Torn pieces of the girl's map were strewn about his hiding place, but he remembered the dance studio was only three blocks away. Leaving his tarp, he ran, cutting between delivery trucks, crouching behind the auto parts store, and risking a dash across the gravel parking lot of the Upscale MiniStorage next to The Snake River Dance Studio. A converted Victorian with a gated fountain garden, the studio had ballet slippers penciled on the window of its peeling front door. A bird squatted in the filthy birdbath, soggy black leaves stuck to its feathers. Maybe it was dead. Maybe the sub solar point opened a portal and eviscerated its insides.

"Who is Dr. Jim? You were dreaming. Calling out some guy's name. Jim who?"

He was buried underneath a pile of worn patchwork quilts, and the wood floor was making his hips ache. Sensing mortal danger the moment he heard the girl's voice, he grabbed his rope, pulling the coarse braid tighter. He had been dreaming about an orange solar storm overtaking the lower end of 21st, nibbling up the concrete and asphalt as it raced toward Dave's Pawn Shop. The corn doll had let him access Dr. Jim's four perfect satellites with their thin rod arms flying in tetrahedron formation, a mere six miles apart, searching in 3D.

"Where am I?" He pulled the covers over his head.

Dressed in a pink leotard, tights and ballet slippers, her brown hair twisted into a tight bun on top of her head, the girl patted him on the head and softly whispered, "It's me, silly. You know, your friend."

"The green girl?" He lowered the quilt.

"I like that. I'm going to tell Mrs. Holland that you called me the green girl."

The seventy-two-years-old Mrs. Holland had watched *Stripland* engulf her hillside home with its views of the canyons and crevasses rising to the Palouse Prairie. Her father was a Presbyterian minister who had made the mistake of sending his only daughter to Sarah Lawrence College in Yonkers, New York, where dance reigned supreme. For sixty-one years she had lifted wrists and twisted ankles in the Snake River valley to make beautiful shapes out of young girls, feeding their ballerina appetites until they popped with the obesity of hamburgers, diet coke and candy bars.

Unlike the others for six decades, her latest protégée was fearless. Mrs. Holland had warned her. No visitors. It was their secret alone if she slept on the dance studio floor. The girl's parents were horrible people without taste or vision, the mother alcoholic, the father greedy. Sophia had finally found her precious pearl, and she wasn't about to ruin it.

The man with the rope tried to sit up. A few inches from his feet, a long mirror reflected a pile of bedding and the looming figure of an inquisitor dressed as a dancer.

"What's with burst mode?" she insisted. "You kept blabbering about Dr. Jim and burst mode like you were my science teacher. Are you a scientist? My father told me that not all homeless people were bums. Some were people who gave up. He knew a man once who was a big shot businessman who lost his wife and kids in a boating accident. And he gave up. Lived in some alleys back of the bank he used to own."

"Don't talk to that man," screeched Mrs. Holland, racing across the wood floor, her thick, thumping heels driving fear into the man with the rope.

He scrambled up before realizing his rope was so twisted around his waist that when he lunged forward it spun him a complete 360° before flipping him backwards into the mirror.

"Don't scare him!" the green girl shouted.

"Step away from that man! The police will be here any minute," Mrs. Holland ordered, picking up a long mop broom and shaking it in the face of the dirty, overweight man sleeping on her highly polished floor.

"Are you okay?" The green girl was unwrapping the rope while trying to get her friend to stand up. "You have to go, quick. Quick. Follow me."

She bolted toward the back door of the studio, pulling the man by his rope, his thick neck and bulbous head hunched over his bowed shoulders. His left leg limped. Blood oozed from his left hand.

"You old witch," the girl screamed as she helped the man down the back steps, across a back driveway and toward 17th. She pointed at a clump of bushes in front of a forested area at the edge of 18th Avenue where the concrete blocks of the shopping center, home of Macy's, JCPenney, Rite Aid, and WinCo, created a bunker and set of terraced steps he would have to scale.

Before he dared make a run for the hillside, the man and girl huddled together in the thick bushes, watching the squad car pull up. Mrs. Holland waved her arms in the air and pointed towards the scrap of woods.

"Go back." The man with the rope pushed the girl and pointed toward her teacher. "She wants you, not me."

"I'll try to find you," she answered, walking backwards away from him.

He scurried away under the brush, more like a large animal than a man. She could see the bushes shaking for a few seconds, then nothing. She caught a glimpse of his rope squirming. In another minute, the hillside had swallowed him.

Two police officers were running toward her as she slowly walked back to the dance studio.

"He's gone," she said, unrepentant. "He didn't hurt anyone. No one. She shouldn't have called you. He's a good person."

The police were not impressed. For a few minutes they tromped around in the bushes with their nightsticks, hitting branches and sending tiny birds flying in all directions.

"I hate you," screamed the girl at Mrs. Holland.

Mrs. Holland realized the police would have to make a report.

"It was a big misunderstanding," she said once the police officers returned. "I thought it was a vagrant, but it turns out it was only a school friend of my student, my prize student. Would you like some coffee? I have plenty of muffins inside, big juicy huckleberry muffins. Could you pretend this didn't happen? I'm so embarrassed."

The man with the rope had dived under a downed tree and could peep at the police from his hiding place. They kept asking Mrs. Holland questions, and she kept touching the arm of one cop and pleading, her body shrinking.

He whispered, "Stay still. Don't say a word."

:: EIGHT ::

The man with the rope stank of *Stripland*, rotting ketchup, sticky fingers, and thrown-up blizzards. Teriyaki sauce dripped down his tee shirt, long squiggly brown lines, crisscrossing bloody dots. Stuck between a six-foot pile of neatly folded cardboard boxes and a rusted dumpster, he chanted, "Swallow sounds." Fumes from a tossed can of gasoline made him think of his sister's garage where his old Buick was parked. The smell made him gage. He bit hard on his lower lip. No sounds.

At the far end of the shopping center parking lot, he heard TV noise from a lone RV. Shots fired. Screeching brakes. Then laughter. Head toward the laughter, but not too close. Don't let them smell you. Past the RV, he sidled down a steep incline into the brush-filled ravine, scrambling along a dirt path toward Henry's old camp. Henry told him the story about the deserted camp soon after he came to the blue house. Cougars chased the men away from their hiding place since they had to avoid where 21st Street turned into Thain. Too many cars. Henry thought cougars might tunnel underneath the busy highway like Jerry wanted to do. Enter the safe world underground where hunted animals find haven: bobcats, gray wolves, and badgers tucked in dens. Big long claws digging tunnels. No cars. No cops. No shooters. No trappers. Henry said the cougars still roamed the ravine, searching for rabbits and stray deer. Henry was trying to scare him with his talk of his two weeks close enough to the Nez Perce Grade to hear the rumble of engines and the snarl of the big cats. Stay clear of the marshy areas, Henry warned. And rattlers in the dry upland. Watch out for their slinky babies ready to strike.

"It was a young cat, but big," Henry said. "Long, long, long tail and attitude. Looked at me like I was nothing. Like the people on this street look at me. Not even a nod."

The man with the rope didn't believe him. There weren't any cougars left in the ravine. They probably sensed the disruptions in the magnetosphere with special brain cells like the ones found in sea turtles or migratory swans. Animals and plants were smarter than humans. Stuck inside their electrical machines, people couldn't sense the magnetosphere. He was lucky he found out when he did. He too could be roaring past on Thain blind to the geomagnetic field lines. One woman interviewed at the decommissioned Hanford Nuclear Reservation believed that if she couldn't see radiation from the nuclear tests, it didn't exist. She probably didn't believe in magnetic lines either and was trapped eternally in visible light.

"A large boulder, halfway to the bottom of the ravine," Henry said. "Behind the boulder." Henry was emphatic.

Henry lied. Not like the corn doll, but like the people at Mental Health Court who told him he would be okay if he came to every meeting and listened to the therapists and reported over and over again for two years, letting everyone standing or sitting in the courtroom—even those men with the guns—know what he was supposed to do and if he did it, then they would give him free movie tickets for the 12-Screen Village Cinema or a coupon for Wendy's even though he liked McDonald's better and never went to those dark rooms that blasted big pictures and made his ears hurt.

"A large black boulder, you can't miss it," repeated Henry.

And he didn't. He almost ran into it in the dark, his face stopping just in time to throw up his hands. He searched behind the boulder and found a pile of dirty toilet paper. It stank worse than the dumpster.

But smelly didn't kill. He was safe. No cougar.

Resting against a downed log, the man with the rope listened to a swarm of insects buzzing. Away from judges, doctors, therapists, and the police, he finally felt at peace. Bugs were better than people. Covering his legs with leaves, his rope safely at his side, he closed his eyes and forgot the two men chasing him, their bulky guns on their belts, and the police man with the gun firing, his face a terrible mystery like the magnetosphere. Dr. Jim could not measure it. Only corn doll could trace accurately the fissures of hate, fear, humiliation, anger, and disgust to map and decipher his face.

The tin buzzing faded into the chatty calls of birds. Breathing came easier. A tree shook in the wind, raining down catkins and drying leaves. He thought about staying, for weeks or months, and living like a fox or coyote. He might make it.

Then the night fell asleep.

Muffled thuds woke him. Heavy feet. Feet with shoes.

Quickly, he swept more leaves over himself. Camouflage, Jerry used to caution, it's the homeless man's friend.

The thuds stopped. There were no sounds, not even the dead leaves moved. Then the bushes came alive with lights. First one boy, then two, then three. Giggling boys. Until one tripped over his knee.

"What the?" Flicking aside the leaves, he shouted, "Fuck, a dead retard." Skinny tall with a fat face, he sniffed and snickered, "No, a stinky retard."

"A homeless retard," said the second, laughing as he bent close to the man with his flashlight. "Man, look at this ugly guy."

The third burly boy didn't smile at all. He pushed the other two away and inhaled a big whiff. "Virus, virus," he moaned, clutching his throat and throwing himself on the ground until the other two grabbed hold of him, laughing like three baby boys that the man with the rope had once seen in a day care center when he lived in Flagstaff, Arizona.

The man with the rope smelled the beer and felt better. People who drank beer liked to talk big but usually didn't hit.

"What the fuck is this?" The second boy reached down and picked up the end of the rope. "A tail," he laughed. "We caught us one with a tail." Yanking hard, he ordered, "Give it."

"No," yelled the man with the rope, wrenching his head back since his rope was twisted around his neck.

"Mine."

"Mine?" mimicked the burly boy. He looked at his two friends and threw down his can of beer.

The man with the rope was not tall, but he was thick and stout with a bulldog neck and a shiny head.

The first boy moved behind him and grabbed the rope, twisting the man's neck, making him teeter on the soles of his feet. The boy was pulling him hard, choking him.

"Let me have some," the second boy yelled.

"Give it to me," the burly boy ordered.

Hesitating, the first boy loosened his hold, and the man yanked his rope away, freeing his neck.

"Mine," he screamed.

"A fuckin' rope," laughed the burly boy, amused at the response. "What do you do with that dirty rope, old man?" he asked. Then he whispered something to his two friends.

The man with the rope tried to walk backwards, his feet pushing away the brush and branches, their flashlights blinding his eyes. He could not see the two other boys, only felt the burly boy poking him and shouting in his ear.

Then he felt them plow into him, throwing him flat on his face in the dirt. They held him down while burly boy sat on his back, bouncing up and down like he was a trampoline.

"Mine, mine," they were yelling as they grabbed the rope around the man's waist.

"Look at the knots he has in that thing." The burly boy stopped to examine his prey.

"Fuckin' long too."

"I got a knife," his friend added. "Let's cut it off."

Burly boy plopped down hard on the man's back. "Better. Let's tie him up. And call the cops."

They kicked him a few times in the head and rolled him over until the rope was no longer coiled tightly around his waist.

"Prison awaits." The burly boy marched to a large cottonwood beyond the boulder.

Before they tied him to the tree, they had fun dragging and yanking. The burly boy watched as the other two grabbed the end of the rope and pulled as hard as they could until the man shot up into the air. They tied his arms behind his back and twisted the rope around his feet. Each time was funnier than the last.

:: NINE ::

Crickets sang. His hair popped with their churning buzz. Blood stuck to his eyelashes and dribbled down his cheeks, but he was happy. They were gone and the no-people quiet brought cool air. Breathing to check if his ribs were broken, he made a list: no deep cuts, facial lacerations, or punctures. He could see, smell and taste his tangy blood, but the rope was still attached to his waist. He could wash it when he was free. The rope would find a way to release him. He only had to wait.

The boys would never call the police. They would run home and smile at their parents.

Tied to a tree was not terrible. His wounds could rest, and the MMS might float past with its antennae arms, searching for ruptures in the magnetosphere. From under the cottonwood, the full moon cast its long shadows on the rough hillside. Faint headlights glowed like comet trails from Thain. The Milky Way flowed across the sky, a Celestial River, a phrase the library astronomer repeated when he showed slides of the sun's ferocity. But inside the twinkling river of the galaxy, neutron stars and black holes ripped apart solar systems, star clusters, and spiral arms. It was more like hell's highway than heaven's river. Chance cosmic storms could vaporize the ugly electric monsters outside of town on the parched hills by the Indian graves, plunging the town into darkness. Our lives depended on the MMS and Dr. Jim watching for breaches in the earth's protective fields projecting plasma to blow up satellites and disrupt GPS until no one on earth knew where they were or where they were going.

Looking through the tree branches, he spotted the constellation Cygnus at the meridian, flying like some lovely swan and hiding a huge galaxy filament, the burial shroud of billions of stars, planets, and life-forms, reduced to dust, spitting out muons at any unsuspecting passerby, especially those new planets discovered by NASA (Not A Single Answer) that the astronomer bragged about. Bragged! Planets orbiting around stars about to implode, explode or collapse into black holes, beaming X-Rays, Gamma Rays and Cosmic Rays!

"Get me out of here," he screamed, surprised at the sound of his voice.

He looked down at his shoeless feet, his head collapsing forward, every joint ached, his legs throbbed, and the light from the moon was green. He could smell fur.

First the cinnamon nose, sniffing the air, came right up to his face, then the long white whiskers brushed against his lips. One big bite and it would be over. No more face. He had always thought it would be a solar storm.

The broad bronze head sloped back into a deep set of pale blue-green eyes, ringed with delicate white fur with an eat-you stare, no Disney blinking kindness.

Henry was right. There were cougars in the ravine.

"Hmm," the man whined, a pathetic sound from deep in his throat.

"What happened to you?" the large cat asked.

The cougar squatted down at his feet and started to lick his toes.

"Please don't," the man whispered.

"Your toes are covered in sores. I always lick."

Plopping on its side, the great cat stretched and yawned, opening its mouth as if trying to decide what to do.

"There's a reason for everything," it batted the man's feet and sniffed his ankles. "Please," the man whimpered.

The cougar slowly arched its back, rose, and paced around the cottonwood tree three times in a clockwise direction, examining the ropes.

"A conundrum."

After another excruciating circuit, the cat stopped. Its long, pointed teeth tugged at the stubborn rope. With anti-gravity grace, it then jumped on a thick branch above the man's head and looked directly on his bald top. The long tail floated down, and the cat's curved claws disappeared into its thick brown paws.

He could hear the cat breathing and sense its calculating stare. Why was it taking so long? Was it playing before the kill?

"I'll do it for the corn doll," the cat purred, giving the man one long lick across the top of his head.

With a growling roar, the cougar leapt off the branch and into the night sky.

The man did not move. It could be a trick. He stayed frozen until his numb left hand fell at his side. With some gentle twisting, he freed himself from the tree. The cat was gone.

Winding his rope back around his waist, he tried to move, but his right knee buckled. Filthy and covered with bruises, he limped toward the lights of Preston Avenue. He trudged past a prickly bush, its thorny branches a haven for wayward bags from Safeway, Walmart, and Winco. His lead legs stumbled on the litter-sprinkled path. Styrofoam snowflakes clung to his pants. Empty Mars and Milky Way wrappers stuck to his soles. He trampled a Coors can, an empty pack of Orbit gum, torn Want Ads, a single $2-off coupon for Naked Juice, and an assortment of blue, pink and yellow plastic caps covered in dog poop. He reached Preston, crossed, and hid behind a row of manicured shrubs.

Random luck: the Subway Volvo idled in the Moneytree parking lot.

"Don't worry." Al, the Subway man, comforted him. "Nothing seems broken, but you have to get that dirt out of your wounds. Those head cuts are teeming with germs."

He proposed driving the man with the rope to the Mormon church where he could use their basement shower. It was either that or the hospital.

"No hospital," the man insisted.

"Okay. Do you want to call the police? Take some photos of your injuries? Who the hell did this to you?"

"No hospital. No police."

The Subway man had been fired or "let go," though he kept insisting to upper management that there was nowhere to go. His food-giveaway did not go unpunished. Luckily, an old colleague found him online through a series of random accidents and offered him one semester of teaching remedial math, or more politely Basic Mathematics, MTH 06300, at a community college in Michigan. When the man with the rope staggered into the Moneytree parking lot, Al was waiting in his car to secure a loan with his auto title, the only thing he owned: $500 at the reduced APR of 202.11%, down from the ordinary installment load of 323.96% so he could buy gas. Kirtland Community College in Roscommon, Michigan, needed his services fast. If he drove for 31 hours straight, he might make it to faculty orientation.

"I'm going to slip in Boolean algebra and Venn diagrams. I hear undergraduates are addicted to binary digits they can't recognize. If it doesn't work, there is always another Subway."

The man with the rope settled into the Volvo like a familiar couch, his body hurting from head to foot. He had to trust someone. No stories about cougars. Only the night boys. Keep it simple. Kicking and pounding. No licking.

He didn't want to go to the Saints. They parted ways a few years ago. The church had abandoned its old beliefs and was now into Captain Kirk and happy endings. Only if they gave him a pair of seer spectacles would he do anything for the church, help with open houses, door knocking, and fried chicken picnics. He had read about the old one's sunstones with their marble eyes and parted lips, probably talisman against solar storms. The original Saints knew something about the cosmos. They didn't care about real estate holdings or running for president of the United States. Like the corn doll they believed in visions.

"Don't worry about it." Al sensed the man's hesitancy. "I don't believe much either. One guy came into the store a few weeks ago and thought I was a Shoshone and started asking me to picnics in his backyard. When he found out I was Chinese 100%, he hesitated but shook my hand and said I could come anyway. The Mormons love those Shoshones and even some of these Nez Perce if they can catch them. I'm simply using their extended facilities for a short while until I get out of town. If you sign on, you get a crap load of stuff. You should think about it. You need medical help and look like shit."

Al pulled a pair of pants and a clean blue tee shirt out of his backpack and handed it to the man with the rope.

"No worries. Let's get your wounds cleaned and bandaged. Then I have to get on the road. Someday I will find you again and you will tell me the entire story of the rope. Don't worry about the magnetosphere. There are worse problems. If someone starts asking you to spell words backwards, run. Run like hell."

:: TEN ::

"No lights," whispered Al. "Give me the end of your rope."

It could be a trap. The man with the rope never let anyone touch his rope unless it was a kindly woman on the bus. And then he only let its tip touch the heel of her shoe. Al might yank him down the stairs or tie the end of the rope to the railing into a trick knot, then call the police. You could never be too careful. He wrapped the rope around his neck and cautiously pushed his foot forward until he could feel his toes come to the edge of the step. He counted fourteen steps straight down to a pitch-black basement.

The darkness made his body hurt, his stomach heaving bitter juices. Maybe Al was an undercover saint sent to lure him into a subterranean room for a preemptive baptism before he died. He'd heard about baptisms of the dead in basement temples and wasn't taking any chances. He held the end of the rope tight against his chest with his left hand, clutching the banister with his right. Even dead people were not safe, though he thought they might have some supernatural strategies to avoid involuntary immersion. He had to remind himself that the Saints today were more like accountants filling quotas, spiritual debt collectors that used smiles to enter your name in their ledgers. They had to create Excel spreadsheets to justify what they did. Maybe counting was safer than having visions. If you had a vision, they killed you. Look what the anti-Saints did to their Prophet in Carthage. Shot him in the back. His followers had to hide his dead body from the mutilators.

If you had a vision, never tell anyone and definitely don't write it down. A mob would come and kill you. They would hack, burn, stone, drown, waterboard, slice, behead, shoot, hang, nail, bury, starve, flail, skin, puncture, beat, and whip to death. Look at the trouble Joseph the dreamer had with his brothers. He narrowly escaped death.

His high school friend had a vision, and he was shot dead seconds later. If you can't shut your mind, at least shut your mouth. No secret writing either. It didn't matter if someone else showed you the vision like an angel, a talking god, a dark star, or a celestial snake. Shelve it. No sharing visions. Period.

Corn doll never talked out loud. She was smart. And the cougar? He'd never say a word about the cat.

Safer to keep ledgers with neat columns and count names with incentives like free bus service to ball games and Christmas bazaars.

"What is taking so long?" asked Al. He didn't sound angry, only concerned, even worried. "You need my help, and I have to get back to Moneytree before they open."

"Why do you have a key?" the man with the rope asked.

"Eddie, the part-time custodian, said I could use the basement in an emergency. Why? Don't you want to wash your cuts and take a shower?"

Al had turned on the light in the bathroom at the end of the long basement. The man couldn't see anything in the room resembling a small pool or large font for cleansing souls. As he walked toward the light, he smelled the dried blood on his face, the garbage splattered on his ripped clothes, and his rope smeared with dog shit. The night boys were probably home sleeping peacefully. They would not remember him. At least, they didn't get his rope.

Al had turned on the shower water. Stone-green girl wanted him clean. Henry wanted him clean. His sister wanted him clean. Clean was more important than visions to most people, maybe even more than baptism. He remembered how hard he worked to get that McDonald's coupon from the judge. He had to go to the therapist every day for a month, except for the weekends when the house monitor watched him. He had lists of things he had to do in every pocket before he could get the coupon. At the top of the list: take a shower.

"Is it a trick?" asked the man with the rope.

"No magnetosphere can reach down here. You're safe."

Al might know mathematics, but he didn't know solar storms. The earth would be scorched. Every living thing burnt to a crisp and everything humans built vaporized.

"Is there a Celestial Attic?"

This was a trick question. If there were, he would scramble up the stairs as fast as he could and walk to the pawnshop. Even the cougar understood his mission. If not, maybe Al was helping. A Celestial Attic would be the worst place in a temple to experience a solar storm. It was a front seat. Dr. Jim probably knew about Celestial Attics since they might open portals for plasma. The Prophet and the old Saints didn't properly understand the ferocity of the cosmos. Their universe with its billions of planets promised infinite space for soul-settlers to find peace and love. They turned their eyes to the sky. In 1844, the evil earth people chasing them, burning their houses, and murdering their families caused them to find comfort in the stars. But they knew nothing of the sun's fury. Our solar system housed a dragon spitting solar storms.

"A what?"

"Not too hot." The man with the rope answered. "Do you have an extra pair of shoes?"

Sterile gauze pads were plastered up and down his arms, legs, and back. Sitting across from Al, the man with the rope smelled of lavender soap and Desert Essence shampoo. He gathered his rope in his arms and examined how clean the braiding was after the scrubbing. He raised the tip of the rope to his nose and sniffed. He was clean.

Al searched through the kitchen cabinets. Every hotdog, hamburger, pack of potato chips, bag of apples and carrots was gone from the refrigerator. The open house had cleared out the temple. A lone banana cream pie sat on a long table next to a 2-liter bottle of Diet Coke Caffeine Free. Al handed the man a long plastic milkshake spoon.

"It's going to be close." Al zipped open his daypack, pulled out the pages of his Moneytree contract, sorted them on the table, and calculated the first day of his payment and the first day of his first paycheck.

"Maybe they have a Cash 2 Go in Roscommon that I can leverage. Creative financing could be a subspecialty in Math 06300. I might even set up a website for the kids."

"Do they only come for the food? Why didn't they eat the pie?"

"Because it tastes like artificial sweetener. No, it's not only the food. They need an anchor. You have a rope. They don't. It's that simple."

"It's the sacred grove." The man with the rope ignored what Al had said and instead remembered the vision received by the Prophet in the green woods. "My friend knew a medicine tree close to Cottonwood Creek. I went there once with him. We drank and he told me stories. He's the one who told me about corn doll."

"Corn doll?"

"I can't tell you anything. But I will ask her about your paycheck."

Al laughed and pushed the pie closer to the man with the rope. "Eat more. You must be starved."

"You don't know anything about this temple religion, do you?"

"Not really."

"My friend knew. He told me that their Prophet's visions were like those of his tribal dreamers but with no jokes or tricks. If you were staying, I would take you to the tree."

"Can I drop you somewhere?"

"He's dead. Shot five times. Not as bad as a solar storm."

"Sounds pretty bad to me." Al jammed his papers into an outside pocket and looked at his watch.

"Remember the temple last night? Its lights shimmering, its wings spread out like the flying swan at the meridian. The needle tower, an antenna listening to the stars?"

He explained to Al that when the entire satellite system of the United States failed, the church would still have a high tech communications network. Salt Lake City could still listen to the cosmos. He fretted that his friend should never have left the protection of the church. When his friend turned twenty-seven, he went on the reservation road through Utah, New Mexico and Arizona, hoop dancing and playing the bone game. Maybe he should never have come home to Idaho. His friend worked as an EMT and what he saw on the highway brought him horrible nightmares. Visions were not nightmares. His friend had visions too and spoke one out loud and that's why he was shot.

Al had not heard the man with the rope talk so much and felt uncomfortable listening. Too much crazy talk. He went in back to turn off the lights. If God existed in whatever wondrous forms, mathematics must be the language God spoke, provided the Great Number One knew the Greek alphabet. The thin bio-skin of the earth grew billions of years after space-time burst from a mathematical formula.

"Visions might be some crack in space-time," he said out loud.

When he went back to the kitchen, the man with the rope was gone.

:: ELEVEN ::

Covered in a thick film of gritty dust, the pawnshop's upper windows cast lurid yellow light on stacks of VHS tapes. Inside, early-morning customers compared brittle revolvers laid across a glass countertop. To the side of the front door, a row of six cracked recliners was occupied by old white men who went dead silent when he tugged his clean rope into the store.

He scooted fast when the guy in the upholstered rocker asked if he would trade the rope for a gun.

"I could use that rope," he said, poking his friend in the side, gesturing with his coffee thermos to the cracked gun case at the north end of the shop. "You go over there and pick out a sweet gun. For under $25, that is. If you give me $24 and that rope, I'll give you that gun. Not a bad deal. You could always shoot yourself with that gun, provided you buy some ammo. A lot better than hanging."

The row of friends shook their heads in agreement, egging him on.

"Wait a second," he added. "I've got a better deal. I can just take that rope off your hands. You might hurt yourself with it. Me and my friends, we'll take care of it right nice. Right, fellas? Need to test out my new knife."

The man with the rope ignored their snickers and walked to the cash register where the owner was leafing through a thick catalogue.

"You finally came back," the owner said, glancing up at the man with the rope, scanning his face.

The man with the rope looked along the back wall behind the long, gray-haired grizzled owner and leaned over the counter, checking every inch behind and below, leaning in so far he almost flipped on his head.

"It's gone." The owner closed the gun book and glanced up at the man.

"Liar," he responded, sitting down on a stool in front of the glass case where the corn doll used to stand, propped up on a metal ring holder.

"Did you hear that, Dave? He called you a liar?" Chortling, the guy in the cracked orange recliner hit the sides of his chair.

"Stay out of it, Mel. It's a private matter."

The man with the rope didn't move and Dave went back to reading his catalogue. A few people drifted in and walked the gauntlet of retirees before deciding not to buy anything. The decrepit store hoarded junk, broken and dented by lives long gone, an RCA flip-top TV, a roll of used vinyl flooring, cardboard boxes of garage tools, dusty mounds of up-ended kitchen drawers, and broken guns. The man with the rope waited, trying not to make eye contact with Mel who watched every move he made.

"Is Axe going to sell that .38 Smith & Wesson?' one of them asked.

"Yeah, what about Sam's Remington? He promised me that old pump-action," another added.

"Worth shit," the owner responded. "Not like this puppy." He stooped behind the counter and brought out a Heckler & Koch MP5. "Picked it up from an old SWAT team friend of mine."

Dave pointed the gun at the man with the rope and then swept it over to the row of recliners. "I want you all to leave right now."

"Fuckin' shit," said Mel. He stood up and stared at Dave to see if he was kidding.

"Fuck if we come back here again."

"Get your sorry asses out," yelled Dave. He pointed the gun at the man with the rope. "You, stay."

After the store emptied Dave came back to the counter and set the gun down. He went back to reading his catalogue.

"Is this a hostage situation?" interrupted the man with the rope.

Dave didn't respond. He looked as if he was never going to respond to anything ever again, not his squawking grown children, not his pissed-off wife, not his medical bills.

"Can't think it through," the owner finally said. "I locked her up."

Dave looked at the back room.

"She started talking one day and won't shut up. She used to hum this strange soft singing. I could never make out a word. Then last week every word became a bullet. Told me about Bear Paw and how she used to live with some little girl a long time ago. How this little girl held her so tight, her fingers froze around her until someone came and pried them loose and stuffed her in a burlap bag. About the scavengers skirting the battle looking for stuff they tore off the dead, bloody buffalo robes and beaded dresses. About a Napoleon gun that blew up the deep pit the little girl was hiding in with her mother." He paused to close the catalogue before continuing. "She's been talking nonstop. Keeps making this horrible cry and I'm telling you, she wouldn't shut up. I had to shut her up. I put her in a gun case and locked it tight, so tight, no one will ever figure out a way to get her out unless they blow it up and then she will explode into a million pieces that can't say shit."

"Is she talking now?" asked the man with the rope, getting off the stool and walking toward the back door.

"Fuck, yes," replied Dave. "Can't you hear her?"

The man with the rope sat down on the floor in front of the back door and listened.

"You have to let her out," he finally said.

"Hell I do." Dave grabbed his gun and pointed it at the man with the rope. "I want you to shut her up."

PART TWO

LAWYER OF IMPOSSIBLE CASES

:: TWELVE ::

She was trained to write in plain style, but her mind bent toward paradoxes, codes, and words left out or erased. Sentences shorn of ambiguity and deception were the supposed gold standard of law, nothing but the truth, and her wealthy clients rewarded her diligent fact-finding rendered in clear prose. Ten years working in a corporate office with polished mirrors larger than her living room floor had taught her that the right document written precisely and filed at the right time with every heading correct was an *open sesame* for the rich, not to mention the offensive strategies of legal briefs, appeals, and pretentious threats sent on embossed letterhead. Some lawyers were masters at intimidation; others were masters at drowning their enemies in paper, full-pressed like an Armani suit, in aligned files, folders, and boxes along with their digital companions poised to overload their opponents.

But ten years was long enough. She stashed her stilettos, transferred a chunk of her money to the Lewis Clark Credit Union, and brought home what she had learned in Chicago. The game was played for lower stakes in Idaho, but it still ended up killing the little guy. No lawyer. Bang, you are dead.

Since returning to Lewiston six years ago, Cass Zinski had worked out of her father's old legal office, not even bothering to redecorate or change his swinging sign. Over time, she had adopted three rules for her practice.

One: Listen.

Two: In ten minutes, if you smell a con, interrupt and buzz Margaret. Margaret wasn't exactly a bouncer, but she knew the bottom-feeders of Lewiston and their tricks.

Three: Act. That was the simplest and the hardest. As the town's designated lawyer of impossible cases, Cass was often the last stop before bankruptcy, eviction, or jail. Her clients arrived at her door ready to scream after a string of horrible experiences and high fees, often left unpaid. Their problems reached beyond the need to sue or obtain relief through the courts. Their anger was a birthright, a lament against the built-in roadblocks to survival, let alone success.

One other point: She didn't need her clients to pour their hearts out, though they often did. They didn't need her sympathy. They needed her legal know-how and tenacity. She liked winning, and she relished upsetting the power guys in her home town. She was like her dad. Once he got his teeth into a case, he would never let go.

This morning a potential client hesitated in her doorway, a petite, skinny woman, who tensed her body, sticking her neck forward and chin up, as if something was caught in her throat. Her toenails, ten blasting pink spots of Revlon's Vivacious 276, stuck out from dirty flip-flops and mocked the pain sketched on her face.

"Sunday, call me Sunday," she said, sitting down with a jerk to her shoulders.

When the words started, they wouldn't stop, a long rambling rant against "lawers." The woman started complaining to Cass that she and those dozen incompetent, conniving members of her profession were to blame for her troubles.

As Cass doodled on a legal pad, she remembered a joke her father used to tell: Satan visited a lawyer late at night and announced that in exchange for his soul the lawyer could win every one of his cases. The lawyer paused a second then asked, "What's the catch?"

Why not blame lawyers?

In another fifteen minutes, Sunday's tirade turned into a bass song, thumping an unfixable complaint, a steady rhythm anchoring her life. "No help," Sunday repeated in sudden, rapid fire, her eyes tiny marbles in wrinkles of sand. "Even that young gal public defender. She set those cops right. But she can't help anymore. Once my brother didn't show up for court and went missing, she told me outright, she couldn't do a thing."

By the end of the hour, Cass had scribbled disjointed notes with circles around the name of Sunday's younger brother, Sheldon, an overweight, partly disabled fifty-seven-year-old white man, a wanderer picked up for vagrancy who periodically refused to stay in his half-way home and had recently disappeared. *Not homeless*, Sunday kept repeating as if that phrase separated her brother from the low-life drifting in and out of the river valley, the druggies, runaways, and young thugs with nowhere to go but settle into an abandoned house or park shelter.

"He scares 'em," the woman said. "Never hurt nothin' or nobody."

Sunday didn't want any favors. She said she could pay. She didn't have much, but she could pay. She wanted Cass to get her brother off the street away from the cops.

"He sees things. Somethin' is wrong with his mind."

Sheldon's sister wasn't embarrassed or humiliated by the disgrace of having a sibling sleeping on brown grass and scrounging garbage. She was frightened for him.

"Somethin' happened," Sunday repeated to herself. "Somethin'. I keep askin' him. Won't tell me. Two years ago spring. Somethin' made him worse. Maybe you can find out."

Mrs. Sunday Deacon didn't wait for Cass's reply but kept talking in a scattered monologue about how Sheldon had trouble crossing busy streets, how there was a stinky ditch off 21st by the Baptist church where she found him once, but she had looked there already without luck, how he had found that dirty old rope in a dumpster behind Safeway, how she hated that dirty old rope, and how he dragged it everywhere with him. Then she finally took a breath and said maybe old William was right: Sheldon saw things most people couldn't see.

Eventually, Margaret peeked her head in the door and said the next client was waiting.

Standing up abruptly, Mrs. Deacon threw a chewed-up file on Cass's desk and stared at her, "My brother needs help."

"I'll do what I can," Cass replied, opening the file.

"Heard that before," said the older woman, as she turned on her heels and walked out.

"Weird stories," said Margaret. "Maybe you should let this one alone."

Another thing about Margaret: She had a direct pipeline to the town's gossip, and since her mom was part Nez Perce, her kitchen table was flooded with rez rumors. Turns out the tribal elder, William Ellyn, wanted Sheldon found too, and that complicated the case.

A friend of her deceased father, Ellyn had known Cass since she was born and was like a second father, a tougher father, teasing her about her fussiness and insecurity. He kept tabs on her when she went to law school and sent her newspaper clippings on tribal conflicts over sovereignty and water rights. When she practiced corporate law, he went silent; but once she returned home, he waited to see how she'd use her legal expertise. He still practiced the old ways when most of his family and friends leapt over each other to escape the rez and its stagnation. William knew its pitfalls but believed he could make life in rural Idaho better, both on and off the reservation. Some called him a dreamer.

The case wasn't just a fetch job, a lost relative easily found at the free food café or in the basement of a friend that needed legal help to get access to addiction rehab or job training. William Ellyn wanted Sheldon for a reason.

"He can't have gone far," said Margaret. "I mean, if you do decide to get involved, how far could an overweight, middle-aged man travel by foot? This town isn't that big. And I know some Nez Perce watching for him too."

That cinched it.

There was no way Cass could say no to Mrs. Sunday Deacon.

:: THIRTEEN ::

Reconnaissance: an examination or survey of a track of land to ascertain the position or strength of an enemy, or the collection of information of whatever kind. Recon is what her vet client, a LRRP (long-range reconnaissance patrol) in Vietnam, called it before he passed away in a VA hospital from lung cancer. Besides orienteering and backpacking when she was young, Cass's skill set wasn't strong on tracking, but she was good at collecting information. Start with the "young gal public defender" and go from there.

First meeting: McDonald's.

Twenty-seven-years-old and barely out of Seattle U Law School, Flora chomped on her Big Mac, alternating fries flying into her mouth and gulps of Diet Coke, her brunette bangs swaying in rhythm with her frantic chewing. "Sorry, Cass, I've just had too many things tossed on my desk. More things on the desk. More things in the mouth."

The crowded restaurant at the foot of 21st had the usual customers at seven am, a mix of bleached white-and-blue collar workers driving either pickups or small sedans. Briefcases sat next to work gloves and baseball caps. Newspapers, torn napkins, and empty plastic cups covered the small tables because there was never enough staff at the peak morning hours to keep up with drive-through rushers and eat-fast parkers. School kids skipped around the customers in line and headed shrieking to the play space. Only the lone man in the corner fixated on his computer screen seemed oblivious to the frantic crush.

It was hard to get Flora to focus on Sheldon. She had her own lament. As a young public defender, she was eager to defend the indigent since 90 percent of the people who walked in the courthouse were poor. But nine months and thirty-four pounds later, she was working triage, barely able to find time to have a junk breakfast.

"Evicted, recycled lives," Flora said, brushing crumbs off her black blazer.

She had proof.

Close to her office, the statue of the lone Nez Perce warrior on his horse watched the poor in front of the county building. When they got off the bus, they stood dazed at the bottom of the twenty steps ascending to the front doors of the courthouse. Many lives ended in prison. She had the numbers. Others were simply struck dumb by the charges and held their breath as they passed the eye of the metal detectors and security guards. She had witnessed the trauma.

Flora's lament soon turned into a rant, listing common, criminal offenses: parking fines, suspended driver's license fines, past-due electricity bills, rent, alimony payments, and outrageous finance fees for payday loans. Zap: go to prison. Even folks who thought they were immune folded. A job and a house one day, the next, a money pit after one bad-luck trip to the casino, the extra drink before driving home, or a medical crisis.

Simple information was not Flora's forte. For fifteen minutes, she repeated out loud what she said to herself at night before she went to bed. She was hitting the wall. The wall of no legal defense and no possible help.

After staring into her Diet Coke as if life's answers floated there and a moment of calm, Flora returned to Sheldon. "I guess the rope really freaked out the white-haired greeter."

Finally, information.

1. Sheldon was facing a criminal charge of indecent exposure for having peed behind Cash 2 Go. No store would let him use their bathroom, and a Walmart greeter had called the police on general principle because he didn't have on a shirt and was dragging a rope behind him. Unfortunately, the police caught Sheldon in the act of urinating.

2. Sheldon was assigned to mental health court, hence postponing his sentence and jail. Mandatory mental health treatment supervised by a judge for at least eighteen months with required transitional-housing. Only then could he get the magic ticket: a get out-of-jail free card, record expunged.

3. Sheldon had spent six months in the first stabilization stage of what was called problem-solving.

4. Sheldon had screwed up big time. He didn't show up in court for a week and hadn't slept overnight in his halfway house.

Tumbling down the rabbit-hole, Sheldon could be anywhere. The adult vagrant had grown up in Lewiston like Cass and probably knew what the daylight people called its dark nooks and crannies. White, middle-class girls like Cass were warned not to wander in the Lewiston night. That's why her parents insisted she go to college in Chicago, a safer community.

"Is he in danger?" asked Cass, trying to unpack why he disappeared.

Flora shrugged her shoulders. "Do you mean is somebody after him? I don't know."

"Is he dangerous?"

Flora shook her head. "He is if you are afraid of ropes." She half-laughed while her left-hand fidgeted with her food and her right checked for text messages. "Sorry, Cass, I can barely keep up. No hide-and-seek for me."

In another few months, Flora would probably send out applications to firms in Seattle and head home, running as fast as she could from the labyrinth the town's poor would never escape.

"His sister wants me to find him before the police," mentioned Cass, hoping this familial plea would jog Fora's memory.

"And you know what I want for Christmas? A bigger budget." Flora tossed her car keys on the small table. "I don't want to sound cruel, but once that bench warrant is issued, your chances of changing anything are fucked."

"Sounds like my kind of case."

"You know this won't generate a dime for you, and there's no clue to his whereabouts."

"Good to know." Cass explained that she was also helping out an old friend.

"Some friend." Flora crunched her empty bag of fries. "Look, this may sound strange, but I really like Sheldon. I think eighteen months of supervision by the court was simply too much for him, and his sister could barely pay the court fees. It's like he doesn't believe he has enough time left. His days are numbered. Not even double digits. If anything, he might be suicidal."

"Any ideas about where to look, besides the halfway house?"

"Dumpsters? He has to eat."

A new reconnaissance job for Cass: dumpster hunting. She calculated there must be a dumpster or two behind every fast-food joint on 21st, not to mention the budget motels, strip malls, gun shops, banks, churches, and payday loan companies. Another thing they left out of her law school courses, checking in garbage bins. Finding Sheldon would involve leg work into what her father used to call the Dante's hell of Lewistown, the franchise rings of neon and bad food.

Flora started sweeping up the scattered crumbs on the table from her hamburger and dumping them on her crumpled napkin. "His sister is useless. Sheldon took care of her for years, sending her money every month from his job in Arizona. Then they traded places. She can't handle him." She crushed her napkin into a small wad, not aware of how much anger she was inflicting on that square of paper. You're going to need help, big time."

Sticking her mutilated napkin into the hamburger container, Flora stopped and looked around the crowded restaurant. "How many of these people eating their McNuggets are seconds away from total financial meltdown?"

She fingered the edges of her Diet Coke cup and whispered. "Damn, I can barely pay my bills. Law school put me in the dark pit of debt. And this job is not going to get me out of that holy hell anytime soon."

Flora struggled to get up from her molded plastic chair, balancing her briefcase, a stack of files, a takeaway snack of apple dippers, honey mustard snack wrap, more world-famous fries, and her collected garbage.

"For later," she grinned as Cass grabbed her arm to steady her.

There were several lawyers in the public defender's office just like Flora. Their underfunded advocacy kept chipping away at the power of the police and state to roll over people when what they needed was dynamite. From their desks they tried to restrain unscrupulous landlords and predatory lending companies that had on their payroll dozens of well-heeled attorneys fighting back. They were an EMT crew working in America's financial belly, and they were well-trained and smart, too smart. With their own pocketbooks empty, the pay of corporate law smelled sweet. Who wants to work that hard for such modest rewards?

The two women exited McDonald's just in time to see a young girl pulling away from her angry mother and pointing across the street. Dark hair buffeting about her snarling face, the woman yanked the girl away from the busy traffic of 21st. "No," she yelled in a boozy voice, shaking the girl's body. The girl swung around toward the McDonald's window as if she was trying to break free.

The mother didn't look like she had the strength to hurt the child, more mouth than fist, but Cass and Flora stopped, uncertain what to do until two men called to the woman, and she dropped the girl's arm.

Flora frowned and headed to her car.

"Call me if you need anything," she said. "Don't get me wrong about what I said inside. I'm not leaving the public defender's office anytime soon. I just want to nail one lousy trailer court owner and get a free ticket into heaven."

"That's a fee-generating case," replied Cass, walking Flora over to her car and placing the file stack in the back seat.

Before she left the parking lot, Flora rolled down her window and shouted at Cass. "Hey, try talking with Judge Fender, the new mental health judge. She might have some ideas about where to look."

That would take time. Too much time. With the police searching for Sheldon, Cass figured she had a couple days at most.

:: FOURTEEN ::

Next to the abandoned Habitat for Humanity storefront, Dad's Tavern opened at nine in the morning, serving cheap cheeseburgers and cheaper drinks until one am. A dark, dirty cave filled with steady alcoholics, the bar housed the perfect bartender who pretended he didn't care though he kept tabs on the homeless and handed out hot coffee and sandwiches late at night when he could. Cass's cop friends avoided the place unless they were doing bar checks, so she was surprised when Blake, a friend from high school and a lieutenant in the county police force, made it mandatory they meet there. Turns out, he was hiding from both the city and county police.

Neither of the them said a word after Blake announced he was on probation. The forty-something cop with a boxy face and guarded jaw didn't want to go into details. Before the news, she figured he might know something about Sheldon since the county cops kept an eye on transits moving through the river valley; motorcycle gangs, ex-cons, suspected drug traffickers, and homeless people camping in ravines outside city limits. His troubles didn't bode well for intel until more drinks arrived.

Turned out Blake did have two pieces of information:

One: There was no activity on the Sheldon's bench warrant.

Two: Sheldon was still BOLO (be on the lookout). No city or county cop had yet spotted him downtown or at the usual hangouts for homeless people: the Salvation Army, a few churches, or the new rescue mission that had taken over the deserted, roller rink.

Since there was no shelter for homeless men to check, Blake had completed his favor for Cass by asking his last friend on the force for help. Now that door was closed. Her plan to use Blake as her inside cop was over.

"Face it, you're going to have to get in your car and drive. Even better, get out of the car and walk," Blake growled as he drank his tequila.

Cass's recon work was faltering. Her informants were distracted, lost in their misery as if the town's problems were running toward them at such a breakneck speed that their only thought was to jump. Pumping them for further information yielded limited results.

Maybe she did need to survey the town of Lewiston to "ascertain the position and strength of the enemy." She needed a new and improved map. She had already driven the downtown streets of Lewiston looking for Sheldon. She knew where the streets intersected, turned into irrational one-ways and halted at dead ends, but she didn't know where overgrown pathways turned into havens offering shelter. She didn't know where homeless people went at night to stay outside of the glare of cops and citizens trained in surveillance through their evening news and internet terror-talk. Her map had hotspots for crime and known offenders, addresses for heated lawsuits over boundary disputes, bankruptcy claims, shady real estate deals, and even dog bites in trailer parks. What she didn't know was where the homeless of Lewiston could sleep or eat without harassment, punishment or fear. Where were their hiding places from their enemies? That is, most everybody who lived in Lewiston.

Before meeting Blake, she had stopped at Sheldon's transitional housing that was close to McDonald's on 21st. Henry Spencer, the self-appointed house-dad, was more worried than Sunday Deacon. He had given Sheldon a cellphone for emergencies but had not heard a single thing. He had driven up and down

21st for two nights, methodically crisscrossing the side streets. He
was going to start driving even later, he told her, even though he
couldn't see well in the dark. But when Cass asked him about specific places Sheldon could sleep or hide, he clammed up. The two
other men at the house, squatting in the living room, didn't even
want to make eye contact. Their map of Lewiston wasn't for out-
siders, especially ones that dressed in pants and blazers and carried purses that looked like briefcases.

She had forgotten one crucial rule of reconnaissance: Dress
appropriately.

After more tequila, Blake tried to slip behind a booze barrier.
So, Cass settled on finding out what the hell was going on with
him. Each question she asked, he answered with a glib smile.

True to her profession, Cass continued her question drill until Blake finally barked. "I don't have a fucking plan. How about
private investigator? You need help, don't you?"

"Give me a break. When do you go back to work?"

"You want to hear something funny? I unloaded on a state patrol guy during our training session on 'Excited Delirium.' Fuck.
Two cops in training on de-escalation techniques, and we're
screaming at each other. A fucking ex-military obedience cop in
my face. Most cops don't listen to a single word anyone says. They
want people to shut up and fucking obey."

This technique had worked for Cass her entire life. She never
talked back, rolled her eyes, or looked down at the passenger car
seat as if she were reaching for her gun. Her hands were always in
clear sight. She had one rule: Smile politely and hand over your
driver's license and registration.

"Definitely PI work for me."

What a joke. Blake was a cop through and through. Cass pro-
ceeded to give him her free, unsolicited advice and told him that he
was running from being a cop. She explained how there was even a
book on how lawyers escaped the law, too frustrating, not enough

money, not enough justice. After a particularly unfair verdict that let her rich client hold onto his millions and destroyed the poor plaintiff for life, she'd read the book twice and realized that, despite this raw act of injustice, she was a lawyer through and through. Justice was merely that illusive ring on the merry-go-round often beyond reach, but not impossible to grasp. But from her high-rise office in Chicago, justice was not only blind, she was dead. To resuscitate her, Cass needed to change her office location. She had enough money. Why not? Blake just needed to shake the inner cop up. Not leave. One of her clients used to be a city cop. He quit when he realized he hated most of the people he was working with and trusted no one. Wouldn't even turn his back on his partner. He took a job with the college campus police and loved it.

"I'm not afraid of anybody at work," replied Blake, his voice disgusted. "I just can't stand that loud-mouthed state patrol officer. One of his buddies shot and killed an unarmed Nez Perce man two years ago, VE, that skinny, old guy. Remember?"

Cass reminded Blake that she was in Hawaii with her grandmother when it happened, but she still heard about it from William since it happened on his property. For weeks, the FBI were all over his place on the reservation. The crime scene was their turf. They wanted no interference from the local police, city, county or tribal.

"That shooting has festered in this town. Divided us up even more. At each other's throats. All I said to this guy is 'back up.' He was in my face, and I said he was just like the idiot who shot VE on the rez. Back up. First rule of working with a potential perp who is drunk, high, or can't comprehend what you are saying to him. Back up. Give him space. Don't touch him. Listen. Listen. God damn, it's for your own safety. That polite bullshit your father told you works only if you are a particular kind of person, preferably white, middle-class and female. No offense. A cop can't afford not to listen. His life depends on it."

Blake got up to leave.

"Not so fast," said Cass. She wanted him to help her out with the bench warrant. If Blake could tell her as soon as Sheldon was picked up, she could at least try to minimize the damage. Talk with the judge at mental health court before she incarcerated Sheldon. Make a case for him. Something.

She wasn't giving up. Her job was to find Sheldon before the police, but she needed plan B. To get to him first, she had to find out exactly why he was running. He could be in real danger. If he was suicidal as Flora suggested, he might get the police to shoot him. A few years back, a local farmer, Seth Johannes, sat in his pickup truck with a gun on his lap and wouldn't get out of his car for the police. No one could get him out of his car until he picked up his rifle and pointed it at the squad car. No one in his family, wife, brothers, or kids thought he would have shot a cop, but he made them shoot him. Seventeen bullets later, he could count on it.

:: FIFTEEN ::

She wanted to ask him about the book.

Sitting on a greasy tarp in front of a small lantern, Cass listened to a man stooped over a small pile of spoons as he cleaned the utensils and hooked them on his jacket. The smell of white gas clung to his clothes. His bedroll and bag of aluminum cups and pans was tossed to the side. A bent paperback of *The Federalist Papers* was stuck in his back pocket.

An hour earlier, she had ripped a board off the alley door of an abandoned downtown grocery store. The entrance door and side windows were covered with frilly-flowered drapery, decorated with drooping bows of blue organdy, scotch taped to ribbons of dusty white satin, a Gothic display of shredded cheer.

Since the windows on the Main Street side was sealed up, plastered with *Keep Out* signs or spider-webbed with duct tape to cover glass cracks, it was impossible to see inside and check if the tip from the women's homeless-shelter was right: the deserted storefront was a way station.

The dark alley had been her only way in.

Jerry wasn't bashful about his past. He hadn't had steady work for eleven years, and with the weather getting cooler he was heading west to the Interstate to hitchhike south, probably Oceanside if he could make it and if he could get past the Caltrans workers clearing out the camps.

"I've always liked Palm Springs, and the cops there aren't bad. They don't like nasty press. Shooting us in the back is bad PR."

The spoon cleaning ritual over, Jerry sat back and opened his bent paperback. He ignored Cass, waiting for her to leave.

"You better get out of here before the others come," he said after a few minutes reading. "One night in here. That's what we have. Cops will be back tomorrow checking."

From the near-dark room, downtown Lewiston appeared like the set of a post-apocalyptic movie, almost everyone dead, and the remainder trying to survive on scraps. The world where Cass went for her double espresso three blocks away had vanished.

"I gave him a map." The stringy-haired man in the flak jacket finally offered as he looked up from his book.

"A map of what?" asked Cass, tucking her legs under her.

"You're not a charity nag, are you? Finished with that shit."

"Do you know where he was headed?"

"Sure. Following the cosmic winds," Jerry said, gesturing to the ceiling.

Reassuring information that made no sense. Maybe it was a homeless code. Cass asked but received a look of utter bewilderment. She could barely keep up with legalese, police jargon, and the court's acronyms. Did the homeless speak another language? Her psychotic clients did. Their visions forced new words. In two years living off the grid, Sheldon had changed his speech, clothes, and food. At least, she knew his past had been squeaky clean. Blake's friend had run a check on him and found out that he had no record with the police either in Idaho or Arizona until two years ago. Then the troubles came fast with a series of arrests for vagrancy and indecent exposure.

"What was on the map?"

"Why are you looking for him?" the transient insisted.

Cass explained how important it was that she find him before the police.

"Fuck, you're that impossible-case lawyer lady. Getting to the bottom of the barrel, aren't you?"

It turned out Jerry knew more about Sheldon than his sister or his housemates. He told her that when Sheldon first came back to Lewiston without a job after living in Arizona for over twenty-five years, he had hooked up with an old high school buddy and planned on looking for work at the local mill or the ammunition factory since he knew how to work with molds for metal and composite materials. He had had several aerospace jobs in the Phoenix area. He never graduated from college but had good paying jobs for a big chunk of his life. His sister had bad health problems. She needed money.

"Tell me about this old high school friend." Cass had read a city police report with its crisp bullet point lists that didn't give her a clue about why Sheldon had drifted from living with his sister to a life on the streets.

One county police report reduced a strange event two years ago to a minimal sequence of facts:

- *S found walking on Cottonwood Creek Road on the Nez Perce Reservation at 3 am.*
- *S confused.*
- *S assessed as incoherent when approached by county police officer.*
- *S transferred to Saint Joseph Regional Medical Center Psychiatric Ward for evaluation.*

The psychiatric unit let Sheldon go after forty-eight hours since his sister signed a statement that she would take care of him.

"What friend?" Jerry asked. There were only rumors floating through the makeshift homeless camps by a transient Shoshone who preached near the Southway Bridge. "*The time is at hand,* that sort of stuff." He claimed there was a white man who could see the dead from the Nez Perce Reservation. Sometimes their spirits made their way to downtown Lewiston and sat at the outdoor cafes after midnight. A white man with a rope. Jerry thought the Shoshone was drunk and trying to scare white people. Probably saw Sheldon walking on 21st and made up a big lie. Trying to pass it off as prophecy. That rope unsettled people.

"The map?" Cass asked again just as the side door opened and three men came in dragging backpacks.

"Got a visitor?" the older man with the shaved head said to Jerry. "Ain't that comfy."

"She's leaving."

"Evening, ma'am," said the younger, a tender man of around eighteen who looked like he should be in high school, not hauling a bedroll into an abandoned grocery store to find safety for one night.

"She's looking for Rope Man," Jerry explained.

"Is she, now?" replied the older man, pointing to the corner where the younger man headed to spread out their tarps.

"Hey lady, do you have a cellphone or a video camera?" asked the young man.

The older man glared at him. "He wants to get on YouTube. Tell his story to the millions of assholes online. Fuckin' out of his mind. His mom chased him off three years ago, been hoppin' from foster homes to juvenile to the streets. You watch yourself, gonna end up doing real time."

"I hear it's not that bad."

"You know shit," the man with the shaved head sneered.

"Try 21st," said Jerry. "I made him a map of the street lights, some places he could hide. Not mind enough left to use it."

"Float right to hell," the older man interrupted. "Days are numbered. Seen it a million times. One last thing to do before the end. That's Rope Man. On mission."

"Yeah, a mission on *Stripland*. I warned him not to go. No good can come from that hill of neon signs full of mercury. Haven of the normals sucking the world dry. It'll take what's left of him. And that ain't much." Jerry shrugged and looked over at the door. He wanted Cass to leave. It was hard enough without her there reminding him of how life could be with a job and a sense of purpose. He could have been a lawyer. Hell, he could have been a doctor.

"Follow the breadcrumbs," laughed the older man.

"Yeah, he has to eat," said Jerry.

"Like dumpsters?" asked Cass.

"I bet you don't how much food he had when he left. Ask Henry. Go back to the house on Green Star. Start from the beginning. 21st. That's the way, not downtown or along the Clearwater or Snake. He's gone to *Stripland*. On a mission. A one-way ticket."

"Damn right," said the laughing man.

As Cass stood up to leave, Jerry snapped a spoon off his jacket. "If you find him, give him this. It's a good one. Got it in Palo Alto."

The elegant tiny coffee spoon sparkled in the lantern's light.

:: SIXTEEN ::

Seriously, a mission?

Her entire plan of search and rescue, followed by effective legal counsel, was upended. If he wasn't running away, then what was he running toward? A mission implied planning and intent, and, the big one, a probable destination. Who went on missions? Christians and soldiers came to mind. There was no such thing as a vague mission, a casual mission, or a half-hearted mission. You went somewhere to do something important. Where in hell could Sheldon be going, and what was that important that he needed to do?

Without any sleep, Cass returned to the halfway house on Green Star and started asking tough questions, the way a lawyer should. While scrambling eggs, Henry evaded every query on her legal pad. He was craftier than the CEOs she had interviewed in Chicago for discovery depositions, answering with brief phrases that concealed information and cut off further lines of inquiry. Meanwhile the other guy sleeping at the house tried to convert her over extra-crispy bacon.

Biblical answers or no answers. Not a scrap of useful information.

Except Henry seemed to think that Sheldon was on a suicide mission. He had to be found quickly. It was a matter of life and death. The clock was ticking while Cass floundered.

Gunning back to 21st with "Jesus Our Savior" ringing in her ears and a sizzling description of the end times in her thoughts, Cass started to imagine *Stripland* blown away like a scene from a

Terminator movie, every store exploding in a blast of glass and metal. The rapture she heard described over scrambled eggs didn't seem so farfetched. What was anchoring this world of fast food and junk goods? The bible guy was geared up for the last days, gleeful even. Maybe Sheldon had some insider information that required an emergency mission to stop Armageddon.

Cass checked herself from going down that rabbit hole by drawing up a new mental checklist: search dumpsters, unlocked cars, park benches, alcoves, boarded buildings, and bridges. There was one problem. That itinerary would have needed a small army to complete. Instead, she decided to prioritize and spend the morning on the garbage angle, shining her flashlight on couches, flattened squirrels, bags of dog poop, dented rat-poison cans, and scary red, Hazmat containers. Along the way, she made a mental note of how many laws were broken in each and every dumpster.

Unfortunately, no Sheldon. Not in, near or behind.

Once, she even tried a new approach and followed her intuition. Dodging traffic on 21st, Cass scurried into a mini-mall anchored by Starbucks, drove around the parking mess of insomniac drivers spilling coffee, bypassed the traffic jam by Jack in the Box, made an illegal U-turn, and parked her car in the mammoth lot in front of Walmart. On impulse, she thought Sheldon might be hiding among a pile of kid's toys like a lost child.

Clearly, she was not a PI. Her reconnaissance was pathetic, her intuitions worse, and she was wearing down fast, an Energizer bunny with near-death batteries.

New guidance needed: Visit William and his wife, Lydia. William had helped get her in this mess. He had to help get her out.

On the way out of town to the reservation, her cellphone buzzed with voicemails from Blake, Sunday Deacon, Flora, and a woman, called Larice Stanwood, who was screaming about an extreme emergency. Most of the calls were just check-ins, but the one from Larice rambled for a full five minutes until it was cut off by a sharp beep. The bottom line: the tribe was illegally preventing contact with specific members and repeatedly chasing her off the reservation. Also, Margaret had left five text messages since clients were lined up in her waiting room: Where was she? When was she coming into the office? What the hell was going on? Hello? and I give up! She texted back: Don't worry.

Halfway up Ellyn's long, curving driveway, Cass's car screeched to a halt. William had walked down to meet her from his house that was perched on the top of a knoll with a deep, Ponderosa forest stretched out to the east. He waved her car over, pointing to a bare spot next to a rusting tractor and then led her out to a hay field down the hill. Ever since she was a child, she had never bucked William. When she returned home and became what her town colleagues called a slum solicitor, he kept close track of who she represented, how many cases she won, and how much she charged for her services. Hell, she was almost forty. It didn't matter. William's eight children had thrown up their arms at his intrusive ways. They had no control over him. How could she?

He insisted that she examine the hill behind his house. For an hour, he paced up and down the slope, pointing out where the FBI set up their flags and numbers. "Here, here." He shook his hand, getting more determined as he talked. It was as if the killing of VE had happened that morning. In silence, he looked toward the distant valley from his property. "Spirits walk right through that creek bed. Maybe VE will show up some night, peeping in my windows, wanting me to do something." To William, nobody had done anything on the reservation. The tribal council was useless. No justice. The FBI rolled into town and out. No justice. The state patrol did their internal investigation. No justice.

After they hiked back to his house, Lydia brewed mountain tea and talked with Cass in the kitchen about how the shooting was a gnarled knot William kept trying to untie. The more he worked, the more the knot tightened. She had never seen him this way. The white police officer had made a choice that ended in a tribal man's death. What did the police officer want? Why not wait for backup? Why did he confront VE? Why did he pull him out of his pickup? Why did VE have to die?

The evidence did not answer these questions. It answered instead the final verdict that cleared the police officer of the use of excessive force. VE resisted the police officer. VE questioned his authority to arrest him on the reservation. VE denied his right to police. And the clincher, VE assaulted the police officer.

Lydia whispered, "Maybe he wanted to die in the face of the enemy."

Not a licensed lawyer, William had studied legal cases on his own for forty years. His living room walls were piled with used books, scrounged from local bookstores and collected from friends, books on tribal treaties, water rights, sovereignty conflicts, federal criminal procedures, and rules of evidence. Others chronicled the western United States, old memoirs and reports going back through the nineteenth century, back to Meriwether Lewis and William Clark, the two most gossiped-about white men on the reservation. Lewis's early death by gunshot and Clark's actions as a vicious slave owner and father of Nez Perce children colored the stories that circulated two hundred years later in sharp contrast to the glory accounts in history books.

At first, Cass couldn't get William to talk about Sheldon. He kept going back to the shooting.

"What's the connection?" Cass insisted, grateful that Lydia was sitting next to her since she kept reminding him that Cass had to find the homeless man. Time was running out.

"People on the rez know about the man with the rope," he finally offered. "I heard he was in trouble. You help people in trouble, don't you?" William went over to the dining room table, covered in documents. "Look at this," he said, picking up a thick file.
"They still want our land and our water. Chief Joseph had it right.
We need a system of justice. Do you still believe in justice?"

He didn't want revenge for VE. No, the law had simply failed.
Only harm remained, causing more distrust and suspicion of the
police. He agreed that VE was drunk and defiant. But who gets
shot dead for that? William wanted a system of justice that examined motives, that analyzed assault, that insisted on reasonable
actions, that treated all people the same. A system of justice that
held both the police and the perpetrator to a high, community standard. Where the scars of violence were not ignored. If he
could only suspend time in that moment before the police officer
pulled VE out of his pickup. That moment. That was the knot he
could not untie.

The connection? He wanted to know what Sheldon saw. The
man with the rope had seen something in the face of the police
officer that night, something that made him run so fast he could
never return to his life.

William walked her out to her car. "Somebody saw him by that
Baptist church, you know, Mount Zion Baptist, off 21st."

Two men struggling in the dark. One insisting on obedience,
the other refusing to submit. One physically constraining a drunk
driver, the other fighting for his honor. One alive, one dead. Cass
was used to trying cases in court before a judge. With work, she
could even the odds slightly between the rich and poor. But William was talking about a different courtroom where the wronged
dead were heard. Where the emotional past haunted the present.
Where history sat as the judge and introduced into the record the

deeds and atrocities of the United States. Cass didn't know if the law that she studied could allow that history to enter the courtroom. Hers had said in thunder that VE was at fault, and lethal force was justified. What's more, it had confirmed through legal arrangements that the reservation was not outside the state's jurisdiction, not a sovereignty within a sovereignty. Idaho state ruled its citizens, period.

And now Sheldon was caught in the state's maze. It was a race against time. If Cass could find him first, she could lessen the state's power to incarcerate. When homelessness became a crime, the only home permitted was prison.

:: SEVENTEEN ::

"Everybody wants to live forever," the skateboarder mused over his selection of sides for his meatball sub. The man waiting for his decisions simply nodded his head as if he had heard every worldview while fixing lunch.

In a hurry, Cass wanted a six-inch tuna salad to go before she headed to the Baptist church. She wanted to tell the young guy with the purple skateboard tucked under his arm that she was going to expire in line listening to his philosophy. Frustrated, she said to the server, "I don't want to live forever. I just want some food."

The older Asian-American man behind the counter grinned.

On impulse, Cass grabbed the photo of Sheldon out of her small backpack and asked, "Seen him around?"

His head popped back, and he said with a firm voice, "No."

After a long pause while fixing the meatball sub, he looked up at her and asked, "Is there something wrong with him? Is he in trouble?"

"You have seen him, haven't you?" asked Cass.

"Depends," he said, reaching for the tomatoes.

"On what?"

"On who you are," he continued, delicately setting the sub on the conveyor belt for grilling.

Cass explained that she was hired by the sister of the man in the photograph to help him out of a jam with the police. He methodically asked her a series of questions to verify that she was a lawyer. Surprised at his interrogation that included where she studied law, when she passed the bar exam, and her fee schedule, she realized the server wasn't who she thought he was. She had no idea who he was, but he wasn't who she thought he was.

"Perry Mason is rock solid," the server said when he had finally told Cass his name.

"I'm not Perry Mason," Cass objected. "He was cool and had PIs working for him."

"Too bad. He always got them to confess. I liked that."

Al rang up Cass's sandwich complete with a bag of Hawaiian Kettle Style Potato Chips Luau BBQ and a bottle of Dasani water.

"Come back after work, say around eleven. I should be done cleaning up by then. And don't bring anybody else. Nobody."

Stark white with a sword-shaped cross attached to its tall front, Mount Zion Baptist was built close to a slight ravine with a murky creek running out of a grill in a cement waterway to prevent the stream from spilling toward 21st, a drainage ditch ringed by a clump of weeds and trash acting as a safety dam to prevent apocalyptic storm water flooding the town downhill. The few bushes at the edge of the ravine provided some privacy for transients, protection from the eyes of the church and the clustered homes.

Somebody could camp there, maybe one night at most. Cass slipped down the slope to check if anyone was hiding out. No one. Only trash, burnt noodles and floating sheets of transparent plastic resembling the wings of angels.

She climbed back out and knocked on the front door of the church. An obese white man soon appeared whose triple chins shook as he extended his hand in welcome.

"I'm Pastor Jerome. Just working on my sermon," he explained, closing the door gently behind her.

Cass attempted to describe her situation. The pastor smiled patiently until her lengthy preamble was finished and then launched into a diatribe about his church's recent struggles.

"It's the girl."

The teenage daughter of one of his parishioners had a good heart but terrible judgment, he warned, recounting his woes about her supposed mission to help the homeless in Lewiston. She was reckless, even pig-headed. His colleague, Mary, had worked with her in the youth group and, despite her protests, the girl had organized the teenagers into a food brigade, sending them out to camps at all hours of the day and night with emergency baskets. Parents were livid.

"Radical ideas," he repeated several times.

The pastor was breathless with stories about Renee. "I stayed here last week until three am on a lookout. She doesn't understand the simple word, *no*. They can't camp in the gulley so close to the church. Not in this neighborhood. Very sweet, but not a lick up here." He knocked his forehead. "I don't want to get the police involved, but what can I do?"

Cass found out that there had been someone sleeping in the ravine recently. The pastor had to go clean up the mess.

"Toilet paper everywhere out there. Look at this church. Neat and tidy, everything in its place. We are a welcoming church, ready to serve our community. I believe there is some trouble at her home. Alcohol. Her mother, I think. That young lady is out of control. I told her parents. But they hang their heads and do nothing."

The timing was right for Sheldon to have camped in the gulley. Cass pushed the pastor until he gave her Renee's home address.

"She's not there," he suddenly added, as if embarrassed. "I hear she wanders at night, sleeps at friends, and has that horrid woman who teaches dance for a mentor. I can't tell you how many terrible things that woman has done in this town. Thinks dance is a path to God."

"Are you talking ill about Mrs. Holland?" A pencil-thin woman opened a sliding glass door in the hallway and glared at the pastor.

"My wife." He stood at mock attention. "Erma."

Her dart-black eyes surveyed Cass and displeasure tightened her lips. "Yes, the wife," she replied. "*The* wife who has to remind *the* pastor not to gossip."

The couple started squabbling about Mrs. Holland, whose address Cass also wrote down in her notepad. The afternoon was starting to shape up as a series of house calls, ending in an eleven pm rendezvous at Subway, followed by a long walk in the dark. From the description of the last homeless person spotted in the ravine, Cass was certain it was Sheldon. Maybe her PI skills weren't that bad.

"Give me a holy kiss," asked the pastor's wife. She winked at Cass and led her into a side office. "I want to show you something."

On the desk was a ragged copy of *The Late Great Planet Earth* amid a stack of pamphlets with glossy colored photos of outer space.

"Why are you really here?" she demanded once the door was closed. "My husband, as you can tell, doesn't have a clue. You're not from Calvary Baptist, are you? They're always snooping about trying to steal us blind. Come on. Out with it."

Cass wasn't going to go through her long preamble again or justify who she was to the pastor's wife. Pacify her. If she had to return to the church, she didn't want a community of enemies to greet her at the door.

"I'm trying to find one person, a homeless man with a rope. That's it."

"A rope did you say?"

Cass noticed that the walls of the office were covered in folk-art landscapes of the Lewiston River valley. Looking a second time, she saw each one had a small figure of Christ hovering over the hillside. The town itself was a heap of ruins with the main hotel burning and the highway cluttered with car wrecks. People were running along the sidewalks screaming.

"It's all about timing," the pastor's wife declared, pointing to a large graph on the opposite wall. "The days of Noah aren't that easy to count unless you have some kind of key."

The graph was a crazy quilt of premillennial, postmillennial and millennial timelines with tribulation hours, days and years plotted out with red bar end-of-times markers.

"We have some very good biometric Christians helping us out. You need visual aids or people get confused about the differences, pre-wrath or pre-trib." She picked up a laser pointer and shook its red dot at strategic dips and peaks on the graph. "You have to help them every step of the way. See," she continued, stepping back from graph and smiling. "Are you interested? I could give you a mini seminar later today. A study group dedicates itself to the timeline every week. You wouldn't believe the progress they have made."

She took a deep gulp of air and launched into a complaint. "That's why I don't understand why Cavalry keeps sending spies over here. It's not as if the rapture has happened. Or I don't think it has happened. Do you have an opinion? Probably not, you look like one of those know-it-all professional women who lead lives of loneliness and despair. Just kidding," she added with a little hop on her left foot as she reached for a large jar of hard candies on the top of a bookcase filled with theological writings.

"My one sin," she smiled and offered Cass a handful of red peppermint swirls.

"Are you worried about Renee, like your husband?"

"Worried about that little piece of work?" Erma laughed and sat down at her desk. "Take it from me, that little cookie says she is interested in the homeless, but she's not. I'd watch my step around her," she snickered, plunking a piece of candy in her mouth.

Pastor Jerome knocked on the door and slowly came in.

"Are you two finished? I need you to help me look up some references."

Erma shook her head and plunked another candy in her mouth. "My husband has no sense of timing. He wants to fill their minds with hope and possibility. Why? We need this entire faith community working on the timeline, even the children. He simply won't focus, wants to keep jawing on about responsibility to others. What about his responsibility to me and the timeline?"

"That's enough, Erma. I'm sure Miss Zinski isn't interested in our theological struggles. You aren't, are you?" he asked.

"I don't have that much time myself. If you hear or see anything about Sheldon or Renee, please call me on my cellphone or at my office." Cass handed the pastor her business card. "I'm working against the clock."

"So are we, Miss Zinski, so are we," Erma added, shooing her husband out of her office.

:: EIGHTEEN ::

Baptists fighting Baptists. Why squabble when so much needed to be fixed in Lewiston? Wasn't that Jesus' mission on earth? Anyway, the dates were always wrong, so why did the minister's wife waste so much time trying to figure out the end-of-times and protect the church's data?

Lewiston was riddled with extreme believers, some religious, some plain garden-variety apocalyptic science-fiction types who saw little green men going through their garbage at night. Cass once represented a man whose neighbor believed her client was an alien and tried ringing his property with lime and practicing outdoor rituals to force him to move. In turn, he blamed his neighbor's paranoia on his satellite disk, beaming news at dizzying, internet-download speeds, sitting atop his double wide, and he wanted a court order to have it dismantled. All irrelevant and inadmissible evidence. What next, city statues about cosmic rays aimed at the center of Jack in the Box?

Wisely, Margaret canceled her appointments with some lame excuse about a nasty flu bug and switched responsibilities, checking for word of Sheldon with the city, county, state, and tribal police departments, gleaning as much gossip as possible along the way. No one had arrested the homeless man yet, but he was higher on the police radar because a parishioner at Calvary Baptist had phoned and reported that Mount Zion Baptist was harboring criminals. Sheldon was spotted leaving the gulley by the church with a teenage girl and later exiting Mrs. Holland's Snake

River Dance Studio. He then headed alone towards the bushes and probably the shopping mall. Two city police tried to find him without luck. Worse, Renee Sundown was missing. With the bench warrant and now the connection with a fourteen-year-old girl, Sheldon was facing real time. Even Mrs. Holland, the dance instructor, was driving around. And, Blake had called nine times and left a message to meet him at the dance studio at midnight.

"I saved some food for you," said Al motioning her to the back-storage room of Subway. "I'm thinking about giving all this food away," he said, pointing to the boxes of chips. "Everything. Even the condiments. Facebook is great for getting the word out. A homeless fiesta, or hey, I could call it a potlatch."

He handed her a tuna salad six-inch on toasted Italian Herb & Cheese bread.

"I added chipotle southwest sauce. You look like you need it."

The usual evasion techniques. Al kept changing the topic, avoiding Cass's questions, making jokes about the food. He opened the freezer and peered in. "Do you think I should start thawing before I give it away or do you think it's better to keep it frozen?"

Al avoided looking at her. Maybe she should just leave. She didn't need more false leads. Rummaging inside a large canister, he started counting the containers of chipotle sauce. He seemed oblivious of her presence. She had a swift intuition that her lawyering days were winding down. Why wasn't she Perry Mason? He always cleared the innocent and snared the guilty, outdoing the police and the prosecutors. He didn't seem to need money and never hassled his clients for fees. Best of all, he had totally loyal colleagues who doted on him. Mason looked like a lawyer should look in his large LA Brent Building office as neat and tidy as Mount Zion Baptist. Not like her in a cheap, generic blazer and sales-rack pants. He helped people out of the worst jams, and they oozed gratitude. Cass busted her ass for her clients, but she never felt like she accomplished much. At best, she prevented the worst and sometimes only postponed it.

Sensing her despondency, Al opened the back door and sniffed the air. "Okay," he said to what Cass thought was someone standing outside. "He stayed out there in my car. Then he was gone. That's what I know."

Finally, a specific location. Asking follow-up questions about where he could have gone, she opened a map and drew circles around the dance studio and the shopping mall.

Al ignored her. There was a long, terrible silence while he opened some boxes and pushed them toward the back door. He tugged and shoved until they were outside, lined up in a straight line from the back door to his Volvo.

"He was on a mission," he yelled back at her. "An important one. At first, I thought he was jumbled up, his mind scrambled. He's not. I read about SGR 1745-2900 last night. Somehow you never think about it. Too scary."

Returning to the storage room, he asked, "Do you think I should give away the cleaning supplies? Do homeless people need cleaning supplies?"

At first, Cass hesitated. "SGR 1745-2900?"

Excited, Al uncovered a large chalkboard and started drawing with a dry erase marker, circles and lines with spiraling waves and shooting funnels. He explained it all. How Sheldon was tracking the solar storms through some scientist. He drew the magnetic field around earth and kissed it. He drew a smiling face on the sun and then covered it up with a nasty sneer. He told her about the magnetar SGR 1745-2900 hovering close to the black hole at the center of the Milky Way Galaxy and how this neutron star was a mega center for magnetic fields so strong they burst out of the solid crust of the star. Energy humans can't grasp. Too scary.

Sheldon was right to worry. What if the magnetic field weakened or snapped or a solar flare permeated the shield?

"Fried. Like McDonald's fries," Al said, collapsing in a molded plastic chair, his handkerchief swiping his brow.

It was true. Sheldon believed in a looming cosmic catastrophe, a doomsday version of the rapture where nobody survives. So what difference did that make? Where was the info on his precise location? Cass needed to find him before earth exploded, hopefully in the next eight hours. She continued to pump Al for specifics. He only wanted to talk about the sun, that G-type yellow dwarf that goes through fluctuations capable of destroying life in seconds if earth's shield did not hold.

"I've checked the math. I'm leaving soon and think the kids might like this doomsday stuff, get them to work on the formulas for star magnitude and astronomical units, get them to figure out the difference between polar and equatorial diameters. Get them into the heat. It's better than zombies or vampires. What better way to keep them listening then focus on the complete utter annihilation of the earth? Here today, gone tomorrow. I'll call it math of the apocalypse."

On the way out, Al handed her his oversized business card. Under his name, food service employee was crossed out. Scribbled in black ink was his new title: *visiting adjunct lecturer in mathematics* with the Chinese character for listen carefully handwritten on the back.

EAR >　聽　< YOU
< EYES
< UNDIVIDED ATTENTION
< HEART

:: NINETEEN ::

Relief: No Class A kidnapping felony for Sheldon. Renee was no longer missing and laughed at the suggestion of forced capture. Still, maybe aiding and abetting a runaway or contribution to the delinquency of a minor hung over his head.

Sitting in the middle of the studio's polished wood floor, Blake was leaning toward the girl as she chanted an eerie song. Her dancer's straight back, supple shoulders and long neck set her apart from her slumping teenage peers. Her green eyes with their piercing black pupils reminded Cass of her grandmother's eyes near death, a floodgate to another world. There were no words at the end, only those eyes lit by an unknown power.

"He called me Green Girl," said Renee. "I danced for him to make him smile. He didn't want me to touch his rope."

"She was singing me a song about finding lost ones," Blake said, almost embarrassed.

"My mother used to sing it to me when dad disappeared, sometimes for days or even weeks. It works. He would always come back."

Temporary or permanent domestic disappearances in Lewiston were common. Walk-aways or walk-abouts, it was difficult to tell. Some ended up in the rivers, clear suicides. Others were spotted in Spokane or Seattle, still more simply vanished. No sightings. No information. A gaping wound left unhealed.

The green girl told them that Sheldon was in danger and needed immediate protection from what she could not say.

Blake's de-escalation training, known in the police business as E-LEAP (Engage, Listen, Empathize, Affirm, Partner), kicked in as Renee told the story of how the man with the rope only wanted to walk up 21st. The girl didn't understand why, but his life depended on it.

"Sheldon needs you." The girl pleaded with Blake, ignoring Cass.

Cass hadn't divulged her earlier information from Al, the mathematician/food service worker, since it didn't fit any standard of proof. What reasonable mind would accept it? And as far as she knew, there was nothing along 21st that was remotely connected to science or cosmology, unless you counted the financial entrapment stores that charged astronomical fees and interest rates. And Sheldon was walking uphill, closer to the sun. Why would he walk uphill? She tried to practice E-LEAP but failed.

"Burst mode," said Renee. "He kept repeating it."

"Like on a camera?" Blake asked.

"I didn't think about that. I don't have a camera." Renee started to pull her hair up into a topknot. She worked swiftly, twirling and twisting in what seemed like one motion until her hair was a neat clump on a long oval face, a picture frame for her eyes.

"He talked about some guy named Dr. Jim in his sleep. Keep going on about burst mode and reconnection."

The green girl provided more information that Cass filed under inadmissible, unless it was to pursue an involuntary mental hold with its required paperwork, judicial, medical and police signatures, Designated Examiners, and final stop in the Orofino or Blackfoot State Hospitals.

Improvising what she called a magneto-dance, Renee swirled, her arms swaying in perfect ellipses, demonstrating how magnetic lines could fire, creating mega-explosions that pummeled the earth. "I love our magnetic field," she exclaimed at the middle of a long leap across the floor.

"Do you think the man with the rope is a scientist?" Renee asked when she came to a stop. "I hope he is a scientist. I've always wanted to know a scientist. Mrs. Holland thinks the path to God is through dance. My mother thinks vodka. My father thinks disappearance. What do you think?"

"He could be in the ravine, Renee," said Blake. "If he is there, we are going to find him. There are only a few places to set up a tent or lean-to. He probably doesn't have enough water to stay long. It's too hot and the creek that runs through is completely dry. Did you give him any water?"

"No. We ran. That mean Mrs. Holland made sure of that. I didn't even have time to give him my candy bar."

"Where is Mrs. Holland?" interrogated Cass, tired of the green girl's antics. The only point Renee made clear was that the man with the rope wanted precise information about the earth's future, not guesses. And he thought he knew where to get them. Farther up 21st.

"I locked her in the closet," replied Renee with not a hint of alarm in her voice.

"You did what?" said Cass. "Where?"

"Off the back kitchen. She deserved it. Anyway, it's more like a pantry with a great padlock."

"The key." Blake reached out his hand.

Mrs. Holland was in quite a state when the door was opened. Blake had to show his police credentials fast since she was bolting to the old telephone hanging on the kitchen wall. His ID seemed to calm her until Renee walked into the kitchen and asked how she was.

"How am I?" shrieked Mrs. Holland. "You locked me in that pantry, knowing full well I was getting you some apple juice. You little demon."

"Serves you right," the green girl replied in a voice so cool it gave Cass shivers.

Blake followed his de-escalation tactics, and in a few minutes, he had them seated at the kitchen table with Cass scrounging in the pantry for some snacks and drinks. Blake had whispered to her that food calms people and nudged her into action. Pretty soon, arguing erupted again between Mrs. Holland and Renee that lead to a merry-go-round of shouting that Blake couldn't stop until Cass intervened.

Sticking her head out of the pantry, Cass yelled, "Cut the crap." Assuming an intimidating lawyer voice, she blasted them with a few facts about how Sheldon was her client and as far as she was concerned, they could all be charged with conspiracy to corrupt public morals and create public mischief. That kept them quiet. Pretty soon Mrs. Holland was sketching a map of the ravine since every fall she searched for mushrooms on its northside.

"Plenty of deer trails Sheldon could follow." Her hand worked furiously penciling in a series of lines.

The dance teacher thought Sheldon could easily survive in the large ravine. There were plenty of places to hide for home-less people in the tangle of shrubs and trees. It was the only place inside the sprawl of the Lewiston that defied the town. Not so long ago, tracks of bears, wolves, and even cougars were found along the creek side. The town's idiotic citizens viewed the ravine as a wasteland, a slice of undeveloped land close to the highway lights.

"It's alive in there," said Mrs. Holland, insisting that Renee go home or stay in the dance studio.

"No way," Renee countered.

First, Blake phoned the city police to report that Renee was safe. He then called Renee's mother and, since she could barely talk on the phone, her words a slurry slurp of alcoholic mutter-ings, he decided to take Renee home after their trek and get a better sense of mom. He was going against the book with minors, but he didn't seem to care. The four of them were cut adrift from the righteous way to act. They had one goal: find Sheldon.

:: TWENTY ::

Anarchy. Not the good kind: enlightened individuals refusing to recognize government, no commander-in-chief, please. No, the bad kind: total breakdown, lawlessness, political chaos.

The foursome had trudged up the hillside behind Macy's, following a narrow, deer trail through prickly, ninebark bushes until they came to a steep incline that sent them plunging down on top of each other. When they started, they shared a purpose, trying to find Sheldon, now they bickered and blamed, not knowing where to go or how to get there. Clearly, someone needed to seize leadership and establish order. As Cass reasoned, she could try either legal persuasion or intimidation. But which one? Blake could flash his tarnished badge; Mrs. Holland her limited knowledge, and Renee her fierce and unpredictable courage. Somebody had to step up.

Cass decided to use fear. That always drew people together. She announced that there were rattlesnakes in the ravine, and they slept coiled under rocks at night. Anyone could trip over a unseen rock and have a pissed off snake take a bite out of their ankle. She spoke from experience, having had a close encounter with a thick, six-foot rattler deep in Hells Canyon. They needed to stick together, watch out for each other, and decide where they were going.

Their group huddle cleared the toxic air. Mrs. Holland admitted that she couldn't remember where the trails led. Blake admitted that his flashlight had toasted batteries. And Renee

admitted to pushing them too hard into a dangerous pace for a
night of scant moonlight. Stepping up, Cass suggested a repen-
tant Renee lead, followed by Mrs. Holland, Cass and then Blake;
together, they head downhill toward the creek bed, a likely spot
for illegal homeless camps.

Cass's law classes had never addressed whether social unity
required periodic, public confessions. Maybe Perry Mason's legal
skill at provoking an emotional outpouring of guilt in a courtroom before a judge was the reason for the show's success for six-
ty years. His client, the person wrongly accused, was always ac-
quitted, but the TV guilty guy ended in jail, satisfying America's
need for a restored belief in law and punishment. Since the only
person in danger of jail was Sheldon, and he was wrongfully accused or more precisely accused of something he could not possibly avoid, who was the real guilty party? The community? The
laws the community passed? The enforcers of the laws? Where did
homeless men pee?

Before she could further develop her analysis, the group split
apart like a broken whirligig.

The girl with green eyes started speed walking, Mrs. Holland
called her protégée a frightening monster, and Blake threatened
to leave them and head back since Sheldon probably had left the
ravine hours ago.

Passing up Blake and Mrs. Holland, Cass grabbed the back of
Renee's tee shirt.

"Wait," she said firmly. "I don't want you in the lead. Do you
hear me?"

Renee turned to Cass as if she was her mortal enemy.

"You don't tell me what to do," she unloaded in her face.

"What is it with you?" Cass demanded since swift interrogation could lead to surprising results. "You aren't telling us everything. What do you want from Sheldon?"

"None of your business," Renee snapped back.

"It is our business." Scrutinizing her face, Cass witnessed her aura of girlish beauty morph into a ferocious mask.

Mrs. Holland caught up to the group and quizzed Renee about why she had brought Sheldon to the dance studio in the first place. What did she want from him?

The two rescuers surrounded Renee and pummeled her with questions.

Renee acted cornered. She slunk back into the bushes and turned her back. Mrs. Holland tried to touch her, but she shrugged off her hand. When she faced them again her mouth was even more rigid with rage.

"I want his rope," she said, spinning out a story that made her sound like a demented groupie.

"Bullshit," Cass replied, her eyes squinting in disbelief. Renee was gaming mental illness. The lawyer of impossible cases had plenty of clients with real psychoses, and Renee couldn't even get close to their fixations. Renee insisted that her desperate need for the rope came from new information about NASA's MMS satellite and how much the magnetic field was weakening over the Western Hemisphere. In thunderous tones, she claimed that Sheldon's rope was a secret talisman against solar flares threatening to incinerate Lewiston, including the dance studio. Only Sheldon knew what to do. They had to find him and figure out what he knew and why the rope was necessary. People were wasting time. They argued and bickered and said stupid things on the radio and TV, and worse things on Facebook and YouTube. That's where Blake came in and then Cass. Blake could question Sheldon since he knew effective, interrogation techniques and, if necessary, threaten him with prison. Cass could back up Blake and convince Sheldon that he better tell all or face severe legal fines, and yes, prison, prison, prison, maybe even for his sister since she could never pay the fines. Only when the man with the rope revealed his secret could he go free. Regular cops wouldn't bother to interrogate, only warehouse him in prison or a mental hospital. They'd sedate him and forget him.

"Adults think they know everything, but they don't. They don't even know about burst mode." Renee collapsed on the ground and let out a long, lingering howl that got the three adults to stand at attention.

"Fuckin' son of a bitch, now what?" Mrs. Holland grabbed Cass's arm.

Afraid to move, the dance teacher promised her protégée they would keep looking for Sheldon. They wouldn't store him like a piece of used furniture.

Cass felt her con meter buzzing. There was something about Renee that didn't make sense. Then it clicked. Her voice sounded like someone else's that she remembered from a Nez Perce fundraiser.

"You're related to Felix Williams, aren't you?"

Renee didn't answer. She seemed disgusted.

Cass repeated her question to the same stubborn silence.

"Let me put it together for you. Is Felix your uncle? I bet he is and that makes you a relative through your mother's side. If that's true, then your mother and uncle had another brother, the man that was shot two years ago on the reservation by the Idaho State Cop."

"Not a brother, their uncle," Blake corrected.

Cass turned to Blake. "And you knew this already. That's what you two were talking about when I walked into the dance studio and that's what you two have been talking about ever since. I thought you were having some heart-to-hearts about the meaning of the universe, but that's not it. You were comparing notes."

"So?" answered Renee, picking up a stick and digging into the grass.

Blake tried to avoid Cass's eyes.

"You mean Mrs. Holland and I were left out while you two carried on some secret agenda? Now it is time to confess."

"There's nothing to confess," said Blake. "Renee's mother is the sister of Felix *and* a relative of VE."

Renee threw the stick down and talked in rapid fire. "Yes, the unarmed Nez Perce who was shot and killed by the Idaho State Cop. That Nimiipuu guy. Since then my father has disappeared for days at a time and my mother drinks even more. The man with the rope knows what happened. He could put that cop in jail."

"What?" asked Cass. There was no way Sheldon was a credible witness, even if he had seen the police officer shoot VE. The reliability of his memory would be blasted by even a second-rate lawyer. One look at the rope and a motion for a retrial based on new evidence would be dismissed.

"Only he knows the truth."

"But the trial is over."

"For you. Not me."

"She's my Maria Tallchief," whimpered Mrs. Holland. "She can get beyond this mess. She could have a dance scholarship to Sarah Lawrence. Leave Lewiston forever."

"I don't want to leave Lewiston," yelled Renee. "You leave Lewiston."

:: TWENTY-ONE ::

The night sky rocked with a star fest, a celestial party of blinking, streaking, and wandering points of white; down below, the foursome agreed to disagree, each member deciding best how to find Sheldon though no one seemed to know what they were doing as they continued to insist on doing it in the dark.

Near the dry creek bed, Mrs. Holland's head tilted back, looking for signs of catastrophe, the lone meteorite plunging to earth or a supernova explosion, heralding doom. Only the International Space Station flying overhead made her question what she was observing. "Do stars move that fast?"

Renee told her to get back to work, and Blake simply sighed.

Ignoring her protégée, the aging dance teacher announced her need to break out of the constraints of Martha Graham technique, no more pointed toes, tight spirals, prissy tilts, and silly bouncing. The apocalypse forthcoming, dance must embrace the earth, feet in rhythm with the heart's beat, twirls creating trance, not twists and lifts straining to defy gravity. Her girls would learn to face paint and make fanciful masks, maybe Renee could enlist her Nez Perce relatives as assistants.

"Shut up," countered Renee who was turning over a pile of broken branches and ripped cardboard boxes, searching for candy wrappers. "He likes Mars bars."

Uphill, Cass was busy sorting through garbage tossed on a clump of bushes; a half-stuffed mattress, a broken suitcase stuffed with bike parts, tent poles wrapped in a long rope twisted around an out-of-date Idaho Code Citator, a blue-and-white cooler, three grimy blankets, a dog bowl, a stack of plastic buckets, and a dented, propane canister. From the layers of dust and grime, the litter looked as if it had been tossed weeks ago, if not months. If she was an archaeologist or CSI member, she could probably date every piece and record detailed evidence. Interpret the crime scene of illegal trash. In fact, the entire ravine off 21st could be considered a crime scene: an off-limits hiding-place for people accused of drinking, doping, loitering, panhandling, defecating, urinating, molesting, and stealing. A jungle of gutter bums.

Her clients cursed the town's anti-camping regulations that forced relatives into niches that the police periodically searched, unless they received specific complaints, usually irate suspicions from a taxpayer about a homeless person without any sense of responsibility or discipline. If you listened to the local news, the worst-case scenario for normal people with homes: An army of the homeless, shiftless, drug-addled men, carrying filthy backpacks, black garbage bags, and ridiculous signs, threatening social order. Idaho's solution: round them up and punish. The slogan tough-on-crime, an Idaho mantra running through the state capital, the city governments, and the police, justified prisons sprouting like mushrooms in the state. Maybe the expense would make Idaho go broke and declare bankruptcy, and no one would come to their rescue since the federal bankruptcy code could not legally provide relief. Busted.

Surveying the dump, Cass was surprised there weren't more tents in the ravine or an elaborate underground tunnel system that homeless vets had dug to escape capture. But such speculations didn't get her any closer to finding Sheldon. If you are running after someone who is running, you don't know what you are doing, unless you possess intel.

Back to work, she pulled hard on a braided, gold cord attached to a partially buried, plastic bag. A dry cloud of mummified shit puffed in her face. Cringing, she yanked again. Maybe dope. She wrapped her fingers in some tissue from her pocket and slide the red zipper tab open, letting the small, plastic container drop out. Marked "migration box" in black, it contained several large Band-Aids, two miniscule bars of soap from Comfort Inn, nail clippers, anti-fungal cream, a sewing kit, an empty book of forever stamps, a card with the quote: "I will give you rest (Matthew 11:28)," and a folded postcard of a mountain stream with no message but a name and street address: Philip Waylon, 2389 Damon Avenue, Deer Park, WA 99006. The name and address stopped her. A relative? A friend? His own name and address written down so he would not forget? She was rooting around in someone's life. Garbage, coated with trauma, loneliness, and the need to survive. And, the big question, why was the migration box left behind?

Frustrated with her homebound mentality, Cass was about to give up her search among the debris when she heard a growling, more like a metallic snarl, in the outcropping of rock behind her. A silhouette of a long tail flickered above her head.

Freezing, she didn't say a word, but keep repeating, God damn, God damn to herself, and other equally useless thoughts like maybe that's why the homeless guy ran and left his shit behind.

Blake finally wandered by and asked what she was doing.

"Did you hear that?" she whispered.

He hadn't heard or seen a thing and neither had Renee or Mrs. Holland, though talk of a cougar didn't help the group focus. So, when Blake said, "Sheldon is long gone. And, anyway, I can't see a damn thing out here," everyone agreed.

Before they started their hike out, Blake had a few things he wanted to say to the group about the basics of policing. Their lack of focus and inability to think like a homeless person was severely hampering their pursuit. Without food, water, or shelter what options did Sheldon have? He ducked into the ravine to avoid the police, but he wouldn't have stayed long. They needed to move beyond their rescue complex and become problem-oriented: identify patterns and gather community-based intelligence.

Wrapping her blazer's around her waist, Cass set to work, texting her network of clients, legal aid attorneys, public defenders, and friendly police.

"It's the middle of the night," Renee groaned.

Within minutes, Cass's cellphone rang from a caller she didn't recognize. Al's excited voice spilled over his words in such a torrent that Cass kept interrupting him with a long series of slowdowns, and whats. He'd just heard from a homeless guy at the Suds Laundromat off Thain that the man with a rope had busted up the perpetual gab-and-crab session at the pawnshop near the top of Thain, and the furious owner, no police needed, please, had taken him hostage.

Finally, a precise destination. But Al can't be serious about the hostage rumor, thought Cass.

She told him her location at the south end of the ravine and warned that there were three other people with her. He suggested they hike to Preston where he could pick them up and take them to the pawnshop. He'd bring along a bunch of sandwiches and chips. Not much was left since he'd already given most everything away. Fortunately, he'd held back some food just in case of emergencies. He could get there in fifteen minutes, tops. The pawnshop was technically closed, but they could reconnoiter and figure out what they were up against. He heard another rumor through the homeless grapevine that the customers had been driven out of the pawnshop at gunpoint. Not a good sign.

All they had to do for fifteen minutes was find some shelter from the main road since the city cops liked to patrol Preston for the odd drunk or vagrant. They had to get out of sight until Al came.

Slightly downhill was a clump of locusts.

"There." Blake headed to the trees.

"Not back down," moaned Mrs. Holland.

They hunkered under the locusts without a thought for their clothes since they were filthy and disheveled, stuck with gooey Pepsi lids, Happy Meal stickers, and an assortment of dipping sauce containers. The cool grass gave them unexpected relief.

No one said a peep until Al drove up in his ancient Volvo stacked with cans and boxes in the back.

"You can all fit in," he yelled from the driver's window.

Al tried to cheer everyone up and handed out sandwiches and apple juice boxes. Even with food, they huddled in a cloud of resentment.

"I have a sack of plums," Al said, sensing the nasty mood that hung over the foursome and wasn't going away.

Mrs. Holland grabbed one and handed it to Renee.

"I hear crazy things happen in that ravine. Did you see a ghost? I hear there are ghosts down there. And cougars, big ones with glowing eyes."

"Nothing. No one." replied Blake. "A fucking, homeless ghost town."

:: TWENTY-TWO ::

Jammed into the back seat of Al's Volvo, Cass felt something bulky under her butt. She was sitting on an oversized book, *Elliptic Curves, Modular Forms, and Fermat's Last Theorem.* She yanked it out and handed it to Al.

"I wondered where that went," he said, cradling the book like a child. "Pure beauty. Do you want to borrow it?"

The group was headed toward total meltdown. Alarmed about their next move, Cass poked Blake and wanted to know what their plan was. In no time, the group divided into activists that wanted to storm the pawnshop and pacifists who wanted to gather as much info as they could until dawn came and then calmly approach the front door and knock. Cass sided with the pacifists who were losing the battle to Renee and Blake, whose frustrations with his job and their aimless search-and-rescue mission had spurred him into action. Before any more talk, the activists were out of the car, gesturing wildly to join. In horror, Al crouched behind the wheel, regretting he had picked them up but relieved he hadn't said a word about the man with the rope's shower in the Mormon church basement.

"Don't you know what the phrase 'at gunpoint' means?" he asked, having rolled down his window and stuck his head out at Blake. "I don't see a gun on you and you're a cop."

"Ex-cop," shot back Blake.

Renee couldn't be bothered with the irrelevant discussion about weapons and walked straight up to the front door and kicked, sending the security door flying inwards.

"Karate," she said. "I haven't been wasting all my time on ballet. In this town you need to take precautions."

Blake ran after her with the rest of them falling out of the car
and rushing to the door as if it was a magnet sucking them into its
force field.

Once inside, the darkness stopped the five intruders in
their tracks.

"Now what?" whimpered Mrs. Holland. "No one's here."

"A wild goose chase," said Al.

Renee stomped around the store like a little soldier, her ferocious face sending Mrs. Holland into staccato squeals.

"Be quiet," snapped Renee.

"It's that sound again." Cass alerted the others. "What I heard
in the ravine."

"Maybe it's a cougar," said Mrs. Holland. "It could be
stalking us."

"Excuse me?" Al couldn't believe the logic. "Cougars don't
come into stores. They hate stores."

"How do you know," pressed Renee. "The man with the rope
could walk right up to a cougar and talk with it. He could have a
cougar friend who followed him in here."

It was Blake's turn to shake his head. He walked over to Cass
and together they started methodically searching the store, leaving
the rest to argue about cougar sightings and whether to freeze and
crouch down or stand up as tall as you could.

The two worked slowly, bumping into stacks of moldy hiking
boots, bent ski poles, and smelly canvass jackets.

"This isn't a pawnshop, it's a hoarder's haven." Cass picked up
a long, winding pennant with tattered edges.

"Wow, that's an old Lapwai basketball banner. This wall is
stuffed with old junk. Look at these Wildcat jerseys. They must
be thirty years old. Why keep this stuff? Must be from the 1980s
when the team won everything. The Nez Perce kids kicked ass

in those years. Held their opponents' shooting to under 35%. Amazing. Remember that?" Blake handed Cass a framed photograph of the basketball team back in 1956 with a state championship sign hanging over their heads. "Way back then, they even won state."

Letting his sports nostalgia overtake him, Blake lovingly touched netted clusters of basketballs with embedded Wildcat mascots growling on their surface.

"Maybe you heard this guy." Blake tossed Cass a lone, dusty basketball whose blue and white Wildcat snarl was nothing but a faded cartoon.

Cass tossed the basketball back.

Sheldon couldn't have walked uphill for Nez Perce sports memorabilia. There had to be something else in the store he was looking for or someone he was meeting. Why would the owner chase everybody out of the store at gunpoint and leave Sheldon behind? Cass stumbled over a large stack of Lapwai High School yearbooks and stared straight at a massive back door. She yanked hard and the door slide open, exposing a room whose walls were stacked with Indian artifacts. She'd heard about the people in the river valley whose Nez Perce collections could bring big prices on illegal markets, particular those in Germany. But this haul went way beyond the set of arrowheads or spear points. With the light from the street lamp outside shining into the high windows, she could make out a cradleboard, dozens of beaded bags and gloves, embroidered knives and gun sheaths, a few painted parfleches, large hide suitcases for carrying household goods, an exquisite deep red horse mask that she thought about stealing, a line of tomahawks and axes hung on nails like garden tools, a rack of deerskin shirts and dresses, and a spectacular deep green cotton dress covered in elk teeth. It was a Nez Perce treasure trove.

Cass slowly fingered a child's moccasin while Blake simply inhaled and huffed.

"What a cover," said Blake. "Who would ever guess there were millions of dollars' worth of goods inside this rat hole."

By this time Renee, Mrs. Holland and Al had made their way to the back room and were straining their heads to see inside.

Al walked into the middle of the room, scanning the shelves. "I have to tell you something," he said apprehensively. "Sheldon did talk about this place, but it didn't make sense. I was trying to feed him and right before he went to sleep, he started blabbering about Dave somebody and how he had kept a corn doll in a prison, a doll who knew everything about the magnetosphere."

Throwing up his hands, he continued, "I mean what would you do if someone said that to you?"

"The magnetosphere?" asked Cass.

"A corn doll?" asked Renee.

Al confessed that he hadn't been exactly honest with the group. It was time for full disclosure. He'd helped Sheldon more than once. He found him at the Moneytree, or rather the man with the rope found him. That's how Al knew about the cosmic countdown. The man with the rope had to free the kid's toy before it was too late.

"Too late? What the hell does that mean?" Blake stopped bouncing the basketball.

Al never found out about why too late or when too late because he lost the man with the rope. He simply vanished without a thank you. But seeing the loot locked in this room, Al believed Sheldon was in danger.

"We must call the police, or maybe one of those Forest Service people who are sworn to protect artifacts," interrupted Mrs. Holland who was shouted down by everyone, especially Cass who was determined to find Sheldon before the police.

Blake asked everyone to search the room. The pawnshop was a mere façade. Who knows where Sheldon was hidden? Renee raced to a back wall and started pounding as if her karate fists would yield results by their sheer noise level. The racket resounded so loudly it seemed as if doors were slamming throughout the store.

Al found what he thought was a way out of the store behind a decaying upright piano with a six-foot-high pile of newspapers from the 1970s.

"A grave looter," Al exclaimed looking at the headline of one paper that slid to the floor as he tried to move the piano to the side. "Look at these photos from forty years ago. There's that elk dress."

"This is a crime scene," insisted Renee. Helping Al push the piano out of the way, she yelled, "More storage bins."

Blake bumped past her. "What if Sheldon is inside one of these?"

He tried to pry one open when that ominous sound from prison movies echoed throughout the store. Metal bolts sliding into chunky security locks. A lock down at Alcatraz.

Mrs. Holland ran to escape the room crammed with stolen goods, but she was not quick enough. The door slid shut with the resounding clank of metal bars. Everywhere they looked, steel rods had descended, like a precise mechanism inside a clock.

PART THREE

HOOP DANCER

:: TWENTY-THREE ::

Smudged fingerprints ran down the outside of McDonald's west window. The face of the young girl was pressed against the glass as she waved her arms up and down, her greasy fingers painting in long, wavy streaks. The girl giggled. A woman was standing in the parking lot screaming. The tug of wills continued with the girl twisting around, staring in the window, twisting more, a whirling top, hopping and then pointing at someone across the street. She wanted to cross the street, but the woman stormed toward her, grabbing her hard and shaking her shoulders.

Larice Stanwood wondered if the woman was the girl's mother and was dropping her at school early or at a friend, or some strange neighbor who shouldn't be trusted to watch the girl. She worried about the girl. Nothing worked in the world. Nothing.

Every morning Larice drove to McDonald's at the bottom of 21st and sat in the far corner booth for at least one hour, taking stock of her life, fretting. She hated McDonald's, but it was the only place nearby where she could get a cup of coffee at five am. This morning she had looked up the definition of the word *fool* before she left her condo. The word fit her to a T. It was mixed up with a whole bunch of other words like madman, jester, buffoon, dupe and was saved only by the possibility of infatuation. That was she: an infatuated buffoon. Correction: an old, infatuated buffoon.

For two years she had been in some kind of crazy dream, worse than a teenage girl in heat. Lost it. That's what her friends had said. Waking up to her romantic tsunami was painful. A fool to a degree unfathomable. By the time you reached your sixties wasn't passion supposed to be dead? Not true. Desire hunted her down and almost killed her.

When the evening news reported he was shot dead, she morphed into a fury obsessed with revenge. That first night without him she screamed for three hours. A banshee. A woman wailer. She screamed and then set out to destroy the person who took her beloved away. An inner wheel slipped. She thought about killing the cop but decided against it. The desire for a worse fate gripped her imagination. Destroy him slowly. Curse him. At first, she tried her own techniques, hocus-pocus, mumbo-jumbo, and the one her friend taught her, czary-mary, chanted over three photos of the cop that deserved to rot in hell while waving her fingertips to evoke the evil eye and call up nasty pain, buckets of it. She burnt hair, fingernails, little pieces of torn receipts and paper lids from cups of noodles scrounged from his garbage. She tried everything until it was clear: it wasn't working.

So she finally forked over $3,000 and paid for a chance at justice through the magical internet. The price was reasonable. $25 per curse and she could pay with credit card or bitcoin. Easy. She had even spread the curses across five online sites, just in case the delicate, calculated business of cursing missed its mark. If she had more money, she would have done it up right and put out more bucks for a plane ticket to Hong Kong and paid upfront for a big, juicy million dollar curse, guaranteed. Even with the curse club rate, she only dreamed about that gambit, stuck as she was in a crappy little Idaho town with limited means to travel.

The interior of McDonald's shimmered in the morning light. The girl had kept skipping no matter how mad the woman got. She looked like she was singing or humming and did a cart wheel in the parking lot, her pink sneakers a spinning Ferris wheel, before she climbed inside the dirty car. Maybe the woman wasn't her mom. Maybe it was an abduction. Larice couldn't decide and sat eating her Egg McMuffin wondering if she should get up and go outside and question the woman or call the police or sit still and worry more about how she couldn't tell what was happening.

Slightly overweight and *getting on* as she liked to say, Larice was early retired from her job as a part-time photographer at the *Lewiston Morning News* and had hundreds of black and white negative contact sheets in three-ring binders stacked in her closet to prove she had lived a productive life. Above her out-of-style blouses and skirts rested a long shelf with her Pentax, Contax and Leica digital, costing more than anything she owned, including her car, and accessorized better than she could ever imagine.

Why she stayed in town after the killing was anyone's guess. She knew she was a bit player in the tragedy of a town that didn't get how it was damned to hell ever since 1803 when those dumbass employees of Thomas Jefferson, Meriwether Lewis and William Clark, lied and cheated their way across the land mass that is now the US of A and made ridiculous promises while they ate dog meat instead of fish to the horror of everyone watching two Virginians get lost on their trail of deceit. Conjurers and con men on government pay. She had taken too many photos of the town's foolishness to think otherwise. She was one fool among many. She had proof.

On days of despair, Larice supported a grassroots movement to curse the entire town, hoping that would help her get revenge in the stinking hell hole that never glanced at the past because it was too fucking horrifying. Another proof: her neighbors at night watched zombies devour the living on screens small and large. Only in sleep did they descend into their night frights in rem land where they were chased by demons who also wanted payback and rightly so. Talk about images worth recording.

To maximize their effect, one hundred curses were purchased, one hundred punches in the face, didn't she wish. The problem was how specific to get. She had spent hours trying to refine her curses before she pushed any one-clicks. She discarded dozens, especially ones in the category of diminished capacity, like hair falling out since everyday that's happening to millions even without chemo. No, a curse she reasoned must be a poem well crafted, the product of inspiration and venom, catching the exact right words to spin the spell, the details dazzling.

For days, she was carried away with the possibilities. Try as she might, she couldn't stop herself from the thought of cursing everything, the entire town and its fake memories, its walkways and underpasses, even its gnarled backyards and concrete driveways. Curse every drinking fountain and toilet, public and private. Curse the casino and all-night restaurants. Curse the churches, both humble and grand. Curse the police stations, jails, and light twirling squad cars of bullets and dash cams. And in particular curse every living room, bedroom and kitchen, and all the inhabitants therein.

Her imaginary escapade into cursing her desperate neighbors had left her exhausted. Still, sitting in McDonald's, her coffee warm, the dawn engulfing the orange vinyl, she felt the twinge again to clean the land of them for good. Utter destruction. Let them check Facebook then. Stare at their photos of waste and devastation, not those smiling, cute selfies to the camera that they believe are their lives. Let them fall into the super void of cyberspace that they cling to like rats. The problem was the troubling word, *everything*. She kept reminding herself that no animals, wild or otherwise, could be included. No insects or worms, nothing subsoil, or in the wind or air. She couldn't shake her love of the hills and how the rivers converged at a right angle in the middle of town that kept her taking snapshots of green ravines and lonely pine trees on scabby slopes. And there must be human exceptions, like that young girl in the pink sneakers.

Larice laughed at her demented enthusiasm. For two years, she was carried away by the power of cursing. One time she had even inserted a special provision for everything her townspeople had made that was mechanical or needed electricity. She abandoned that approach because she didn't want to be labeled a Luddite. That would be inaccurate.

She was simply gleeful about the possibilities of cursing everyone in the town, not just the state cop, but everyone he knew, loved, or had taught him. For a delicious moment, she was tempted to curse everything the cop bought and everyone who made what he bought. May they cease to eat, drink, sleep, sit, lie, defecate or piss. She hesitated over destroying their souls since she firmly believed that the soul can never be cursed, only perforated and injured. The town's soul was bent, kicked, warped, and pulverized through neglect and ignorance of the melodious collage of intangible yearnings. No music there. No conversing in resonating notes, only mp3s blasting in eardrums blocked.

It had taken tremendous effort to stay focused on the cop who had actually pulled the trigger. Her fury spread too far. Her hatred had grown like a giant mushroom, nourished in the night by decaying leaves. She had watched for one day too many the folly of her town that applauded when a man in uniform stepped out of his patrol car, dash cam recording, yanked her lover from the driver seat, and shot him dead, five times.

She had bought one hundred curses. And not a single one had worked.

:: TWENTY-FOUR ::

"You're turning into a scary lump."

Eleanor taunted Larice, shaking her head as if she knew since they were tiny tots it would come to this sibling meltdown. She'd agreed to meet up with her younger sister before her committee meeting at Mount Zion Baptist and was already impatient to leave since McDonald's coffee smelled of French fries.

Eleanor's mascara stuck in thick globs to her eyelashes, her lips frozen into a tight perpetual smile. Her steel-gray hair reminded Larice of a motorcycle helmet. The recent death of their mother had meant more time together, reinforcing how they disagreed on practically everything. Eleanor was in love with a Baptist god. Larice was in love with a dead man.

Still, the younger sister yearned to share her recent break-through. She had come to understand that falling in love was about slight gestures, the incline of a curved neck with tender intent, the slope of a hip that dips in welcome, and the momentary flash of a brown eye dancing. Such beauty was how Larice came to know love, its swinging bells resounding, unaware that its joy hovered in a moment before gunshots.

She wanted to tell Eleanor the story of how it started one blazing Sunday at 8:07 am in 1974, an ice cream cone in her right hand, sweetness dripping down her little finger, the smell of sticky fresh peach chunks embedded in vanilla swirl; the exact second her sixteen-year-old-self vortexed into love. Sitting across from her sixty-three-year-old sister, Larice instead plummeted into the chasm of time. Maybe it never happened. Her love could be an illusion. Then the sticky smell of coffee brought back the hoop dancer, golden circles twirling on wrists, figures spinning from ankles, knees, waist and neck, a universe of loops, intertwining to the one-two beat of chanted drums. How she stopped talking as did the crowd, mesmerized by the young man dancing to make the hoops come to life, making them into strings and complex domes, snapping them into a set of wings that flew raven down Main Street. She had come for the horses and saw only the man.

"You're hopeless," Eleanor repeated with an irritated cough.

The hoop dancer's feet caressed the ground, lifted them in high steps propelling him past the sidewalk crowd. There was tenderness after all in men, a disturbing sensation to a teenage girl who counted men she had dated. A chalkboard in the basement listed her pubescent conquests, first names only and number of times; Jamie 7X, Robert 4X, David 12X, Dennis 1X and on. There was a string of 1Xs going nowhere, little experiments that ended after two hours over popcorn, sometimes piling up three names in one weekend because why waste time on mediocre boys? No sex, of course. Not yet, those little pills in her river valley. Tons of kissing, sometimes so passionately she wanted to explode. Restraint was an art without birth control. That time seemed impossible to comprehend. Only the single gesture of a man posed to swirl, suspended in light, resonated true.

"Are you going through another one of those phases? How many husbands can one woman have in a lifetime?" Eleanor was mouthing her favorite sibling accusation. She herself had suffered with one man until he dropped dead at the dining room table five years ago.

There was some truth in what Eleanor said. Larice cringed when she thought about how she relished burning her clothes in between her serial divorces. She'd stand in front of her closet breathing deep and then select the sacrificial item and head outside to the small, rusting barbeque with the convenient black hood, stick the doomed blouse or tee shirt inside, spray it with fluid and light it on fire. She'd stay the entire time, listening to the eager fire destroy a tiny piece of her life, the smoke confined within the greasy hood until there was nothing left but the stink of synthetic or the smoldering scent of cotton. One night she chose a long blue velvet skirt she had saved from her high school prom, shredded it into vertical strips, numbered each one in sequence with a marking pen, and spent a delicious evening burning.

Her life spewed sequential mistakes until she finally understood and accepted that her impossible love was still inside her as strong as the first time she caught a glimpse of him dancing.

"You should never have tried to find him," emphasized Eleanor as if she knew what lay in wait for Larice. "You never have understood men."

After divorce three, Larice had made long lists of friends she had in common with the hoop dancer. At the top was Diane, the redheaded girl in study hall whose freckles practically covered her face. She had no teen-age love and relished romantic intrigues in those vanished high school years. On Saturday, September 29th, 1974, they conspired to eat at a diner in town that mingled red and white in slight variations of color that made no sense since Larice's skin was splashed with ochre and his was kissed with bronze. The abstraction of skin was twisted in a line that wove through the town, threatening and beckoning, an electric wire ready to pop and sting, reinforced by everyone, even those miles away who stayed home and never, ever ventured outside. It bore its way through people just like places, riveting their guts and piercing their hearts, a wire charged. Larice had felt the line vibrate as she walked to the back of the narrow restaurant, past stares and eye blanking the closer she came until she was rescued by an empty booth and spent her first foray into the mysteries of race looking down at her plate of overcooked hamburger, potato salad, and pickle next to a glass of orange soda.

It was a total failure even with adolescent reconnaissance. No eye contact. No nod. Not a whisper or a glance. Her hoop dancer did not know she existed.

Nothing happened until the third try, each time running the gauntlet of blank stares, when the shy dancer walked behind his brother whose voice rang out to his friends huddled in front. He saw Larice then, a warm smile sliding toward her. She took that smile and wrapped it up and carried it in her hand all the way home, stopping first at Diane's to say goodnight. And that smile encircled the moon in 1974.

That's why she had found Diane first. And it was easy even five decades after having not said one word to each other. The virtual trail didn't need breadcrumbs. Diane had moved to Seattle after high school, working downtown selling cigarettes to drunks until a community college turned her into a receptionist in a doctor's office who posted a detailed timeline and photos on Facebook everyday of her dogs, two matched black pugs.

Sidling up to Diane with likes and links, Larice phoned and explained what she wanted. A name, an address, anything to find him who had disappeared in 1975 into the drifting world of tribal seekers, an art class here, a poem there, day jobs to throw and catch until she realized Diane thought her an old fool who had called the Tribal Headquarters too many times, exposing herself to ridicule, if not contempt.

The line reverberated over the phone, sparking and sputtering into every word. And, yes, Diane, had seen him once in Seattle, years ago, at a bar. Surprise. She had walked up to him even with the tribal girl sitting next to him like a bracelet. He didn't want to talk and looked away, not even into his whiskey. She was a zero, occupying no space. And she left without saying one single thing to him. No way, she said, no way I have to take that shit anymore. She'd heard later from a friend that he was enrolled at South Seattle CC in a drawing class. Good luck with that, Diane added. He never finished a thing he started except screwing girls, meaning Larice who hung up the phone after a pause that meant she would never call Diane again.

"I did find him," replied Larice, glaring at her sister.

"The worse for you," Eleanor snapped back. She drew in a breath and motioned to leave. "We have a grief group at the church," she said, moving her large black bag from under the table. "You can't just sit around drinking coffee. I do care what happens to you, believe it or not."

Can you drown in sorrow? There seemed to be nothing to help Larice once the curses didn't work. She had never really grieved for anyone before, not even for her parents or her husbands, two already dead. They simply came and went.

"I'll think about it," said Larice.

"Sure," replied her sister, hustling out the door. She couldn't get away fast enough.

:: TWENTY-FIVE ::

Total inertia. Stuck in place like a beached whale. Riveted to her corner booth. Even the staff at McDonald's was beginning to give Larice the silly looks they usually reserved for transients like that guy with the rope. The tall, skinny high school boy in his red shirt and black cap was mumbling under his breath and glancing over at her.

Earlier, two professional women had been eating breakfast, and Larice recognized one of them, Cass Zinski, a lawyer who seemed to think she could help people in a world that didn't want rescuing. Maybe she should have exempted her from the curses. Maybe her curses didn't work because she had included the innocent and naive. Larice had a few photos of Zinski from a high-profile murder case a few years back. Could she help her find justice? No way, she thought. That never happens in this fucking town.

This morning when Larice woke up, her arms were full of heaving air. A second before, the weight of her lover's body had pressed against hers, his warmth circling her breath. She could still feel his heat inside, her arms empty sticks grasping for an embrace. She had tried to go back to sleep, taking two Ambien to search for him, anything but the old repetition. When she wasn't obsessed with revenge, she tried to figure out why she had lost twice, first in 1975, then in 2014. Why let her find her first and only true love and then kill him? Who was responsible for this wreckage? Two years of wondering why with only online curses to show for her loss made her doubt her sanity.

Abandoned by her sister to sip cold coffee, Larice reviewed in detail her search for the hoop dancer. Did she do something wrong to bring on this punishment? Should she have left her first love languish in her past and not try to find him? She didn't care how many odd looks she got from the teenage workers at McDonald's who kept mopping the floor under her feet. Let them think what they want. She needed to not move an inch from her booth and sort out what went wrong. Was she somehow to blame?

She had first tried to find the hoop dancer through Diane with no luck, only humiliation. Then she turned to Barbs who knew him from church back in the 70s, dreary Presbyterian meetings of converted Nez Perce and a sprinkling of whites living on the reservation. Barbs had heard rumors of course from her neighbors. What could a dancer do in the outside world of buying low and selling high?

The only thing Barbs could remember about her beloved happened years ago when the high school basketball team was hot in the 1980s. Barbs had seen him driving in a brown pickup with a bunch of kids in back laughing and drinking, going nowhere Barbs said as if that three seconds past her house down Cottonwood Lane was firm proof of his degeneration. "No hope for him," she declared in her best Sunday voice, picked up from listening to the same sermon in infinite variations in her new evangelical words: He who denies death and Jesus forgoes mercy and walks past the front doors of his church to embrace Satan. Those who follow not and refuse to eat at the table of the prophets live eternally in hell. "What could you expect," she added with a tilt of her head, a coy look that Larice would store away as more proof that the whole town should be nuked. But Barbs was right about the mercy part.

Her other girlfriends from those days hadn't helped either. She would buzz them and suffer through their chats until she could steer the conversation to the hoop dancer. "No idea," most said until they sniffed out the reason for the call. "Not that old fling," said one, cackling. "He's probably dead on some sidewalk in Seattle."

Were they speaking to her in code? Should she have listened?

Undaunted, she had resumed calls to the receptionist at the Tribal Headquarters that were never returned. They must have thought she was obsessed. Maybe she was.

She had then tried a new approach. She dug out her high school yearbook, a faded blue hunk of paper and glossy photos with odd captions underneath faces now dead, broken with cancer or still smiling as they clutched at their remaining life. She underlined in black felt tip pen three names: James, Ricki, and Santee, the three boys surrounding her beloved at the café where their eyes first meet. They loved him almost as much as she did and were a united front against any incursion into their haven of hunched shoulders and snide syllables, reducing the world to *fuck* and *shit*. Their inside knowledge of his whereabouts might have lasted over the years of having wives leave and kids kick back repeating those same syllables, finding their voice before they walked out the front door, grabbing a backpack or keys to the car. Adios forever.

The local phonebook was never much help, but Larice had tried anyway and was amazed at her success. One of the three friends, James Flowers, was listed, even though she had never run into him or the hoop dancer's buddies for the last forty years, assuming they had fled to Seattle or LA. Maybe he was a returnee, come back to die on the rez and mix their ashes with their ancestors and the sacred land.

Then she had pounced on the first real lead.

Flowers had lived in a neighborhood at the top of 21st past Home Depot, close to the pawnshop she'd never gone inside of except once to check on a steel guitar that she bought and never used, one more peel-away identity, thin as saran wrap and as easy to crumble and throw. She'd thought about bringing the guitar

back only last month after cleaning out her closet of dryer-faded
pants. It had lived in the corner behind the dresses she had never worn in the last twenty years, a good place for a guitar never
strummed or plucked, not once, a dream guitar left unexplored,
shiny white with gold letters.

She had decided not to pick up the phone and call. Too easy to
get rejected. A drive-by was a better strategy, check out the abode
and size up the status, then devise a proper plan. Maybe even wait
around down the street with binoculars to check on comings and
goings and follow discreetly like some private eye, faking a chance
meeting at the grocery or liquor store, a casual run-in. The ele-
ment of surprise seemed to work with those forgotten, the shock
of seeing the young face, old, unglued the tongue. Larice had
needed that chance.

She had bought a Subway sandwich on the way, then stationed
herself down the block, half hidden by a clump of bushes, stopping in front of a white mobile home leveled on concrete blocks
with a long chain link fence running the property line to protect a raised round blue pool resembling a mini oil storage tank.
A curving row of wilted pink begonias made the place look like
home. The house listed for James was pale blue with no fence,
only a dirt brown yard and a dog in the dust.

She had eaten her sandwich slowly, careful not to have lettuce shreds or tomato chunks fall down her front. No one came
out of the house for three hours as she sat in her car, the sun
blasting through the rear window. She remembered worrying
about the dog in the afternoon heat since she didn't see any
water bowl, and the brown mutt had scrunched under the thin
shadow at the rear end of the house. Through her binoculars,
she could see how the dog had its body out flat on the dirt,
pressed against a cool patch. Larice hated a man who didn't
mind his dog. It was a sure sign he was leached of care but still
desperate for love.

Key in the ignition, Larice had gasped when a tall man dressed in a camo shirt and black jeans carefully stepped down the concrete front stairs and headed towards the house next door. He didn't look around, just walked over his lawn and his neighbor's square of gravel and went straight in, swinging the aluminum door hard.

He looked too old to be James, his hair stringy white and a face smeared with puffy folds.

Larice contemplated what her life would be like if she had stayed in the car and not followed James Flowers into his neighbor's home. What if she had never found out that her beloved was still alive and staying on the rez to visit his grandkid. What if, what if, what if.

She kept playing her McDonald's game: What if, what if, what if, each question driving her deeper into the pit and making her admit that there was no way she would have stayed in that car. She had worked too hard to find him again after three marriages and forty-one years of wondering what if. So she had to walk in that house.

James hadn't recognized her even after she explained to him and the guy he was hitting up for cigarettes that she used to "date" the hoop dancer.

He had looked her up and down and saw nothing but a dumpy, old white woman with an Indian guy stuck in her head. He asked her to tell it again and she did and every time he seemed to find it funnier until he was sitting on the couch laughing. He told her if she was a little younger he might take her on. He tried to make her mad and it was working.

"He can't even pick up one of those hoops anymore," he said, wiggling his hips. "Women always want the one that got away." He went on for a while telling her stories about women he'd had and how he was into affirmative action.

She took the abuse. She wanted the address. He even gave her a phone number.

Two years ago, on a hot summer afternoon she couldn't have walked away. There were no *what ifs*. The McDonald's game was finished.

:: TWENTY-SIX ::

The voicemail beeped no-more-time.

"Fuck." She kept talking to Zinski's cellphone anyway, insisting she should be allowed to visit the spot where her beloved was shot. She was willing to pay the lawyer as a go-between to the Nez Perce property owners. And she didn't want any lawyer talk from Zinski about how she couldn't do anything. Blah, blah, blah. Zinski knew the property owners. And she better not use that word, *unfortunate*, to describe the shooting. Losing your credit card was unfortunate. The shooting was unforgiveable.

Larice wanted to throw the phone out the car window but stopped and dialed Zinski's office.

"Don't you dare dump me in voicemail," she said, snapping at Margaret.

"Have you seen the shooter driving around town?" She launched into a list of the places she had seen the cop, out on Highway 12, going up Highway 95 to Moscow, the back road to Lapwai. What was he doing out there? She kept asking the receptionist to explain why he got to drive around like nothing happened. Once she even saw him in the Subway on 21st, eating a bag of potato chips with a smile on his face and everyone in the place was looking at his gun and nodding their heads like he was some big guy in town. He was there with two of his buddies, having fun, going over some car accident that took forever to get off the road. In his version the tow guy was the biggest idiot in town. The cop acted cool, making jokes about grisly accidents as if he wasn't a murdering snake. She wanted to go up and scream at him. Call him a killer, right there, right in Subway with every customer gawking. And why was she banned from the reservation? Who did that?

Margaret didn't say a word the whole time, and Larice wondered if she was taking notes. Perhaps the Nez Perce were making complaints to the tribal police about her. Then she broke silence.

"You have to respect the family's rights. You can't keep going there."

"Is it because I am white?" Larice had tried to be respectful by bringing food and flowers.

Margaret hesitated. "They think you need help."

Larice was sitting in her car outside of Mount Zion Baptist, trying to decide if she wanted to attend the grief therapy session scheduled to start in fifteen minutes. The problem was she didn't believe in therapy. Even the word gave her shivers. Was there a cure for fools? Or, even better, old fools? It was just getting too late in life to get another go-around. She'd had her few hours of love; maybe she should be grateful. Funny thing. She didn't feel grateful. She saw the cop's face late at night and felt rage waves. The cop not only killed her love, he stuffed her with bags of hate. She couldn't see past the fury to feel the love. In the end it was the cop's face dangling that haunted the mad, old fool.

That magic afternoon her lover said that animals were closer to the gods than humans because humans were confused. Long ago, the animals stopped talking with the humans because nothing they said made sense. Human words only made things worse. Word confusion. Words used to make confusion, amplify its sound, agitate its effects.

Larice realized she was still on the phone to Margaret. "I do need help," she blurted out. "Tell them it's okay. I'll stay away. Maybe next month I can come back. I'm heading to grief thera-

py, right now. Tell them that. I want to sit there one more time.
That's all. Maybe in a month or two."

The car door seemed extra heavy as Larice squirmed out of the
front seat and stepped on the hot sidewalk. The temperature was
in the 90s with full frontal sun blasting Mount Zion Baptist, reflecting a white glare that blinded her. She had the sudden desire
to paint the church hot pink.

Once inside, the minister's wife swooped her up and couldn't
believe this was the first time she was meeting Eleanor's sister,
sweet Eleanor, brave Eleanor, Eleanor of a thousand virtues who
wanted the best for her sister. She even put her arm around her
shoulder and guided Larice into a small side meeting room where
about nine women and one man were sitting in a cramped circle.
A peculiar smell hung in the air. Larice couldn't tell if it was candy
or vomit.

The group looked white-haired and haggard. Everybody except one person was in their seventies. Plenty of room for grief
here, thought Larice.

Turns out most of the people had been meeting for over nine
months, regularly. They had a protective feel about them that Larice picked up right off. She and Adele were the newcomers and
newcomers were subjected to entry rituals, like tell your sad story
in ten minutes or less.

Adele went first and announced, "My husband died two
months ago and that same day my twenty-one-year-old cat disappeared." She and her husband had been together for thirty-two
years and had brought the cat home as a kitten. As she talked her
brittle, gray hair seemed to shrivel up. She'd gone all over town
trying to find that cat. She'd finally given up. She had tried a doz-
en things to get her mind to perk up again. Last week she had
taken an aromatherapy class at the hospital and had to leave because the smell of clary-sage, bergamot, and blue tansy infused
with vibrational essences of mountain pennyroyal had brought

back horrible memories of the fights she'd had with her husband.
She missed him like hell. Well, maybe not like hell and maybe not
as much as her cat, but she was staying away from aromatherapy.

"You might try the scent of peaches," another woman piped
up. "Keeps the mind free of bad thoughts."

Pretty soon it was clear that Larice was going to have to say
something so she decided to ask a question instead. "What if what
you are missing is not your husband or wife?"

"That's fine, honey. Greg misses his dog. He had this little
Pomeranian that was the love of his life. Isn't that so Greg?" A
stocky woman named Dorene who might be the leader or guide or
facilitator or elder spoke up.

Greg nodded his head.

"Let's start with a simple thing. I know you're Eleanor's sister.
Everybody here knows Eleanor. Just tell us something small about
yourself like what you like to do when you are feeling good."

"I never feel good," replied Larice, surprised at the truth.

"Why, everybody feels good sometimes, honey. The Lord
gives us these tiny little islands of hope, maybe just large enough
for a finger or a toe. Nothing big. Just small little places to steady
ourselves."

Larice contemplated telling them about her strategy to curse
the town and kill the cop but realized in time somebody there,
probably Dorene, would write it down and call the police. She
needed to prove to the family on the Nez Perce reservation where
her lover was killed that she was getting help. His relatives and
friends had gone through a healing ceremony at a ranch on the
Snake River close to Hells Canyon, some place filled with ances-
tor spirits. The tribe knew how to do death. With over two hundred years of practice, they knew how to keep evil at bay. She knew
only about revenge.

The young woman in her thirties who kept on looking at her
feet surprised the group by asking Larice why she was angry.

"I lost him," she answered. "I lost him to a murdering snake."

"My word," responded Dorene. "Think about the times you had together," she continued. "You will always have those memories."

The rest of them nodded their heads except for the younger woman. "Memories can hurt," she whispered, looking back down at her feet.

"We had six hours together," Larice said triumphantly.

If she had said she had proof that the world wasn't going to end any time soon, and the rapture would never return them to their loved ones, let alone Jesus, she wouldn't have had a more disgusted response.

"Six hours?" they yelled back at her.

"Was that like six hours the last day he was alive?" asked Dorene, trying to smooth out any miscommunication.

"No. Six total hours."

The meeting broke into raucous accusations as Larice was trying to explain how six hours meant more to her than the years she spent with her three husbands, two deceased and buried. When it came out that she was talking about the shooting on the rez two years ago, they turned on her like she knew they would.

"He deserved what he got," said one woman. Another said her son watched the dashcam from the cop's car that was online and knew for a fact the Indian guy was asking for it. The young woman didn't join in. She sat there mesmerized by her feet and then told the group she'd heard about a homeless guy who witnessed the shooting.

"He's crazy now," she said and then got up, grabbed Larice's arm, and walked her into the hallway and out the front door.

:: TWENTY-SEVEN ::

The car windows were wide open, but no passerby could have heard a word the two women were saying. Rosemarie held Larice's hand and whispered about her six hours. In between shallow, heaving breaths, the story of her short life as a mother on earth came out, a slow, hesitant search for words.

"His gray-green eyes opened up so wide I thought I would fall in. I wish I had fallen in. I wanted to die for so long. That magnet I feel every second I'm alive. I'm here. He's gone. Never coming back."

Larice talked about eyes too, how his were warm brown spools of light wandering, drawing her into a buoyant tingling, an energy swell, something she knew was life unaltered, shaped, or bent. There was no before or after.

Rosemarie confessed that her husband was impatient with her moods. He was the one who gave her the ultimatum: Grief therapy at the church or *I'm moving on*. Rosemarie wasn't sure what he meant by moving on since he never moved anywhere except right down the block from his mom and dad, and they didn't want him to move back home. Her in-laws were always dropping by with some excuse to check on her in the evenings after her day job at Cash 2 Go. She interrupted her story of their visits to remind Larice never to borrow money at any financial services on 21st. *Always do without* was her motto. After little Michael's death she knew her life would be a forever *do without*.

Larice took Rosemarie in her arms and held her. They sat in the rising heat without a thought for the people walking past that either tried to look away or stared. One old woman holding a young one, what could it mean? Tenderness was taboo in this rural, western town.

She offered to drive Rosemarie home since the grief therapy session would be ending soon, and she didn't want to see the people who had scolded and insulted her when they left the church. She didn't want to see any of those people again. She thought about driving both of them straight north to Spokane where they could get on a plane and fly to Hawaii. She'd know a lot of people who went to Hawaii before they died. It was like the last chance to see beauty in a sunset or a dolphin's spin before they croaked.

"I think I want to go home," said Rosemarie. "My husband will be showing up any minute. I'm leaving him."

They drove up 21st for a few blocks then headed west on 16th toward the Clearwater River, stopping in front of a small, robin's-egg-blue house with a parched lawn, the paint color more like plastic than the sky. Not one of the homes on the block cared for flowers, only dry, brown grass edged against a strip of concrete foundation running around each house. Curled leaves blew across the front steps where the screen door clanged. A short flagpole with a torn American flag planted in the front yard looked more permanent than Rosemarie's two-bedroom, one-bath ranch.

Larice waited while Rosemarie gathered a few things and came back carrying a dusty green daypack. They drove to the Greyhound station on the other side of the river while Rosemarie called work and told them she had quit. "I have a girlfriend in Sacramento," she confided.

"What about your husband?" asked Larice.

She didn't answer. Instead, she explained that she was glad they had both come to grief therapy today. She had decided to always remember Michael's eyes. She didn't need to forget. And she didn't need just yet to join him.

Then Rosemarie said, "Something else is out there for me. I'm not angry like you. God took my baby. I have no way to get back at him. And I've decided not to hurt myself. God may be a robber and a killer. But I can't kill God. You know who killed your love. And he is a man. I've seen him, trying to get that Indian guy out of his pickup. I watched the dashcam online. Watched it with my husband when I was eight months pregnant. He played it over a bunch of times the first day it went online. You have to promise me something. Promise me."

"OK, I promise."

"Don't ever watch it. I'm telling you. Don't watch it."

Rosemarie made Larice promise three times not to watch the dashcam.

"It doesn't prove anything, anyway. Can't see what happens. The pickup was in the way. All you hear is gunshots."

Sitting in the parking lot waiting for the bus, Larice started to feel her joints and muscles ache. She glanced in the rearview mirror and was startled by how much pain was in her eyes. They weren't anything like her love's. No brown pools swimming in light, only pinched eyes afraid of what they were seeing. She never wished she was young before, but waiting for the bus, she wanted to be sixteen and leaving town, heading not to Sacramento but to Dallas where she would get on a plane and fly to Mérida. She wanted to see parrot colors, emerald green, tinged in blue, and sharp orange reds with yellow tips. She wanted every sky so blue it hurt. She wanted to listen to the sounds of people at night laughing and dancing, not sitting in front of their screens, sullen and withdrawn into pixels, little machine squares dense enough to deceive.

"I'm going to tell you something. I don't want you to go crazy," said Rosemarie, shifting her daypack's strap over her shoulder. "My husband has a friend. He's a janitor at the Jesus Christ of the Latter Day, cleans up the mess from their potlucks, picnics, luncheons, and buffets. He's not a believer though he pretends he is. It's a requirement of the job. He likes to boast about what's going on in the town. A real snoop. Probably goes through the garbage up and down 21ˢᵗ, looking for who's in trouble with the bank or their boss. A real jerk. My husband thinks he's involved with that shooting."

"Involved?"

"Best you avoid that creep."

"There was only one cop responsible. And I know who he is."

"Maybe you don't know everything. You know the guy with the rope, the vagrant that wanders around 21ˢᵗ? He might know something. Heard that at the Cash 2 Go. You can't tell what happened from the dashcam. Not a good angle. If you found this guy, he could tell you more I bet. Most people in town think your love deserved what he got. The cop was polite. Didn't yell at him or scream. Real polite."

This was the first time anyone had talked with Larice about the shooting. No one besides her sister had even known that she loved the dead man. When her friends talked about the shooting, they were thrilled like they won big at the casino, the most exciting thing that had happened in Lewiston for years. She refused to listen to the news or read the paper and never once Googled the shooting. She'd made up a million excuses not to know the details of his death. Told people she was tired of hearing about violence. She hadn't even heard about the cop's dashcam on YouTube. She'd rather spend her money buying curses to damn the cop and the town than listen to their repeat of why a Nez Perce man deserved to die when he was pulled over for running a stop sign and refused to exit his pickup.

Rosemarie told Larice that her soon-to-be-ex-husband couldn't stop talking about the justified shooting. He loved that someone on the rez reported erratic driving to the state police even though they were miles away from the county road. Some *righteous* neighbor looked out her window, knew the car and figured the driver was drunk and disobedient. The dumb Indian deserved the death penalty.

Sickened, Larice hoped Rosemarie would stop talking. She didn't want to know about her husband's death wish for her beloved.

"You need to find the rope guy. I should have told you sooner, but I wanted to get my things and get out of town fast before my husband finds me or I change my mind. Did I say that? I'll never change my mind."

A huge smile radiated across Rosemarie's face.

"Check out the creek wash by Mount Zion. It's okay for you to go back. They're big on forgiveness. Those grief therapy people are just a bunch of losers. They're not suffering. They're there to meet people. Like a meet-and-greet session. Not like us. We had our six hours. They didn't have a second."

The long bus pulled in, its brake shrieking, and a half dozen young people tumbled out, balancing duffel bags, earbuds dangling. Rosemarie smiled wide and her face lost ten years.

"You see, I have my Michael with me." She pulled out a small leather pouch she had around her neck. "I keep some of his ashes right next to my heart."

She waved like a little kid, five fingers splayed, as Larice watched the bus load up the passengers and drive over to the highway to head south toward Interstate 84 and Boise, then farther south and east to Interstate 80 and Sacramento. Rosemarie had described the entire route so Larice could imagine her as if they were together, never looking back, a new go-around on the spinning carousel.

:: TWENTY-EIGHT ::

An eerie, empty light shrouded Mount Zion, shining into its side meeting room with a dull shimmer, reflecting off the folding tables and vinyl chairs that made the parishioners squirm and ache with discomfort on this earth, a positive sensation since their religion defined Jesus as being *very God of very God*, putting him far, far away from these vinyl chairs and closer to where everyone in the church was heading or at least waiting with back pains for the pre-millennial return of this same Jesus. Larice was always confused when Eleanor explained to her the various scenarios for the Rapture. She could be walking around like a dumb bunny when everyone had already ascended or perhaps seen Jesus descend and then ascend along that celestial escalator that her sister believed in completely.

Earlier Larice had stumbled through the creek wash, looking for signs of the man with the rope. One of the neighbors whose second-floor house windows looked down on the gulley yelled out at her, "Nobody there. Cleared out. Are you from the Faith Givers?"

She had climbed up the slick hillside and hobbled over to the older man, his baseball cap smashed on his head so hard it might be fused to his scalp. He told her about how the church was helping feed the transients with beef jerky, granola bars and fruit juice. He'd seen a young girl the other day heading down the embankment. He had yelled at her to get away from there, but she paid him no mind. He told the church about it and they sent somebody down there but they'd cleared out already. It was creepy how those bums knew when trouble was coming. He'd decided to patrol the place. Cleaned up the trash along the creek and kept an eye out from his bedroom window. He didn't want a young girl sleeping out there. "Not good, not good," he kept repeating.

He couldn't tell her anything about the man with the rope. If he'd seen that, he would have called the police for sure, not messed around with the church. "A man with a rope is a dangerous man," he cautioned Larice.

Sitting in the vinyl chair in the empty conference room, Larice tried to believe what her sister believed. Her first impulse was to call up the forces of God to punish the cop. Then she quickly shifted to the devil since he seemed to get the job done faster. *God worked in mysterious ways,* her sister always told her, especially when something bad happened to a friend. This nasty Job-testing God had placed a bet with the devil, so why not go right to the devil and bypass the guy who always had some ulterior motive for hurting people. The devil was more direct. Fewer agendas. By the time she heard her sister's voice in the hallway, Larice had made and broken at least a dozen contracts with the evil one.

"I don't see what mom has to do with this obsession of yours," Eleanor protested.

Larice was telling Eleanor about her hunt for the old transient and had suddenly veered off into a question session about their mother's death.

Their relationship had been in permanent limbo since the funeral.

"I heard what happened at grief therapy. We had an emergency session for three hours last night to undo the damage you did." Eleanor hadn't even bothered to sit down. She towered over her sister like God Almighty.

Larice didn't want to get sidetracked talking about the grief therapy meeting; instead she smiled and imagined where Rosemarie was at that very second, probably in Sacramento sleeping at her girlfriend's after the long ride with her eyes wide open, gawking at the office buildings in Boise and the dry desert of eastern California. She made it, thought Larice, believing for the first time that running from grief might not be a bad idea.

"What did you do with mom's ashes?" Larice asked as if she were an interrogator in a secret CIA prison.

"Why, you know what I did with them," replied Eleanor. "I sprinkled them along that walk down by the river that mom used to love when she was a young girl. You know that. You were there."

Larice bit her lower lip and told her sister she was lying. A gnarly pit in her stomach contracted and released. Their mom weighed almost three hundred pounds when she died. Nobody wanted to even go in her room and change the bed, let alone clean her private business. Her sister had only sprinkled a small bag of ashes on that walkway, not enough to fertilize even one yellow willow those river restoration greenies keep planting.

"Where is the rest of her?" demanded Larice.

"Is this what you call grief therapy, accusing your relatives of evil deeds? You are old Larice. Your mother is dead. Your latest lover is dead. You're next. That's your problem. No Jesus."

Larice started calculating how much she hated her sister. Always had.

"What's this got to do with the old transient? I told you he's probably hiding in the ravine by the highway to the Orchards. Go up there and look for him. Stop badgering me."

Larice wasn't going anyway until she got an answer. Some horrible truth had seized her. She stood up and closed the conference room door, and then stomped over to her sister, grabbing her by her arm. Every hurt and insult rushed out of her as she changed into a large black cloud smothering Eleanor's head. Larice painted scenes describing how a six-year-old girl was thrown out of a red wagon when their mother wasn't looking and how her sister laughed. It was only a fast ride. What's a brain concussion? How she was punched and kicked under the table and threatened if she told about the money Eleanor stole from their mother's purse. How her favorite dress disappeared from her closet and was found years later in Eleanor's basement when Larice went looking for her high school yearbook.

A lifetime of grudges.

"My fault?" Eleanor pulled away and brushed her sister's smell off her blouse. "You're a train wreck."

Larice wanted to choke her.

For a second, Eleanor was frightened. She headed to the door with Larice lunging after her, spinning her around until her sister tripped over her feet and smashed to the floor.

"What do you want from me?" Eleanor cried, her legs twitching.

"Tell me."

"You bitch. Mother never loved you. I took care of her. You were too busy crying over that broken down Indian. I'm glad he's dead."

Those words should have enraged Larice. They didn't. They were the first truthful things her sister had said to her in decades. She drew back and looked at her sister, an old woman, thick and pasty, struggling on the floor, boasting about mother love, pushing her away from the kitchen table, making sure she never got a drop of affection.

"I'll tell you where she is. She's in that big acrylic clock in my house on the dining room table, the fancy one with the bright LED lights that flash. She's in there. Sprinkled in there, suspended in the acrylic forever. I can look at her every morning when I drink my coffee. She'll never get to heaven. I've made certain she'll never leave that clear prison clock. Christ is coming and she'll float sealed inside, shiny little specks of dirt suspended in bullet proof resin that will melt only when the flames of hell engulf her."

Her sister's tears wouldn't stop. For a moment, Larice thought the meeting room would be swept away in the flood.

:: TWENTY-NINE ::

After Eleanor's confession, the two aging sisters sat on the floor of the conference room and hugged. They had spent so much energy protecting their beliefs and shoring up their obsessions about love, they forgot they were almost exactly alike except for the make-up. They promised to try harder, a promise they quickly broke, and parted after a bittersweet embrace with Larice heading out of the church to breath the evening air. Her sister stayed inside, waving at her as she stood under the sharp dagger of the cross.

The hot summer light had faded into a stormy set of clouds hovering over the river valley. Larice thought that the sky seemed to have plenty of room for love even if it was tumultuous and unkind. If Eleanor's Jesus did return, would he take away the constant pain that she and her sister felt? Would she ever see her beloved again? Larice's string of questions found no answers as she drove away, her sister receding into her rear view mirror, a speck that vanished.

She decided to park at the southern edge of the ravine close to where Thain crossed Stewart and figure out if she was going to head down the steep slope to find the transient's camp. She had already driven back and forth on the main road to see if she could spot any colored speck of clothing or tent roof. Nothing. She would have to plunge into the brush if she was going to find the man with the rope. Once out of the car, she walked the sidewalk and sat down behind a convenient bush with her pocket binoculars that she kept in her glove compartment along with the Sig Sauer .380 handgun she had bought last week at the Black Sheep Sporting Goods. She had on her flimsy red flats and calculated her chances of tromping through the ravine dressed in Capri pants, a short-sleeved tee shirt and weak knees. Besides her hips couldn't take the strain.

Her best choice was to park at the shopping mall and wait to see if anyone emerged from the ravine. She had a high beam flashlight in her trunk and could blast anyone coming from that direction. The gun was for just in case. Just in case she saw that cop. Just in case some deranged transient wanted to assault her. Just in case some carjacker wanted her old Nissan. Just in case her life had finally veered into a dead end.

She had a folding chair in her trunk that she set up at the side of the car. The evening clouds parted in small slots exposing the dotted stars lined up to infinity that upset her sense of urgency. The hoop dancer had talked with her about the stars, how he had visited the star man petroglyphs deep in Hells Canyon and knew they were like video messages from the ancient ones, how his relatives had tried to paint the stars on their shirts to protect them, but the bullets of the cavalry had somehow pierced the cloth stars and blown apart their hearts. How military lasers were built deep in the heart of Indian country without their knowledge, weapons made to penetrate the sky, and when that happened the sky would begin to fall, one star at first, then another, then another. Maybe not today or tomorrow or in a thousand years, but sooner than we think, the stars would drop away from their orbits and collapse close to our star and throw our world into despair. She told him the Nez Perce were supposed to be optimistic about the planet. Didn't he believe in how humans might disappear, but earth would last forever. Larice read that in a Native American literature class she took in the 1970s.

He loved her then, took her in his arms and described the journeys he had made since their first love. How he had hitch-hiked his way to New Mexico and studied painting with an old Hopi who let him stay in a back room if he would never drink or take drugs. How those days cleaned his soul and set him back on the right path. How he rode one night deep into the desert and he could hear the stars talking to him about how he had to keep painting what he saw. And how he wanted to do that but what he saw made him not want to paint. He came back to the Northwest and went through EMT training in the evening, every Tuesday and Thursday for five hours and Saturday for eight hours at North Seattle CC, and interned on the highway and in back alleys, but what he saw made him even more convinced we would kill every living thing until nothing was left and then he wandered back to the Arizona/New Mexico state border, trying to find that Hopi man who had gone home to die, but by the time he found him he was already gone, and he finally decided to come home for good and meet his granddaughter that he had never known even existed until his ex-wife texted him with a photo, and to find some peace again, by visiting the star man and listening to his stories.

Larice hadn't realized he was once married. They talked about failure and how nothing they thought was true was true unless it included two things: their love and the love of that eleven-year-old girl who he had tried not to let down like he had the others, a long list of failures that he started to recite until Larice put her finger on his lips and told him he was back now and had felt the love in his granddaughter and they had found each other again and it didn't matter how old they were or how many years they had squandered. There was no arithmetic for life.

Larice wrapped herself in these memories, sensing for the first time since his death that VE was close to her in the night.

It was only when she went to put the folding chair back in the trunk that she saw another car parked in the dark away from the street lights. The driver door opened, and she could see that it was an older woman rearranging piles of clothing inside her white Mercury. After she pushed and shoved bedding, she settled back, reclining the front seat to wait for blissful sleep or something to alter her world forever. Years ago, Larice's uncle had taken his pickup and driven across his ranch to a place no one could find, and he sat there for three days while his family and friends searched town, thinking he had gone on one last binge before the nursing home swooped him up. But they were wrong. He had sat at the edge of his ranch without food or water and waited for the end on his terms. And the end obliged.

Maybe this shopping mall parking lot was where the old people of Lewiston came to die. They parked their cars, turned off the lights, and waited to forget the phony smiles of nursing aides that couldn't get away fast enough from urine-soaked beds. They wanted to forget how the person in the next bed was kept alive by feeding him Ensure until another month went by with a bill for their kids who have to take the payment out of their retirement, if they were lucky enough to have one, and avoid the debt collector, the last vulture of the dying. The peace of the parking lot descended on Larice who walked over to the other car, an old station wagon with a rack on top, piled with a broken chest of drawers.

From the glow of the street lights, she could make out that the woman inside was wrapped in a bulky comforter and stacked around her was a city of dolls, small and large, stuck to the dashboard and the rear window, resting on the insides of the car, small plastic children with perpetual smiles.

Larice tapped on the window and the woman waved her away.

"Don't need any. Go away."

"Just want to see if you are OK."

The woman wrapped the comforter tighter and pulled it over her head, kicking at the door to frighten her off.

Larice noticed that the dolls were arranged in clusters, a trio sitting at a small table, a couple with entwined plastic fingers, a long line of Barbie dolls with hair standing straight up, four inches above their head, as if they had had some awful fright. And one Barbie, crucified.

She left the woman alone, knowing she should help but she didn't know how, and she wasn't going to call the police or the church. She thought about calling Zinski. She might even get the lawyer to come out in the middle of the night and try her famous persuasion. Why not?

She drove to Denny's and made an anonymous phone call from the payphone out front to the lawyer of impossible cases. *Woman in danger. Stop. Lewiston Center Mall Parking Lot. Stop. Come Quickly. Stop.* Then she hung up and drove up the hill past the looming shadow of Home Depot toward the Mormon Temple, not a real Temple like those in Salt Lake City, Twin Falls or Boise, more a meeting house for meet-and-greets with lots of parking spaces for new recruits. She had to find the night janitor.

:: THIRTY ::

Step high, hip, hop, and swing the hoop, jumping, your knees pressed together, then kick and twirl, the loops multiplying two, then four, then eight as you step and touch, small skips, in circles, a butterfly man, an eagle man, above your head the earth perched, a wire mesh of circles entwined, collapsing into wings lifting you above the dirt arena until you rise in slow flight and hover over Thain, a hoop dancer transfigured, light shining through transparent wings, floating over Java Stop, Stinker Station, Papa Murphy's, Dottie's Discount Jewelry, Northwest Title Loans until you come to rest on the pinnacle of the Church of the Latter Day Saints, a transformed angel, facing eastward, glorified.

Larice had a vision. Don't people in grief get sightings? Don't they get to see once more the one they loved? She reasoned that what had happened was not a dream. She had been completely awake, sitting on the steps of the Mormon temple trying to decide if she should try to break in. Her repeated knocking on the doors in the front and back had no effect. The janitor could be inside sleeping or pretending to be asleep.

Frustrated, she started reciting a poem written by a murdered South American poet whose name she couldn't remember. She spoke the poem as if it were an incantation as old as the sounds of the first people conjuring their dead:

You come flying, alone, solitary,
alone with the dead, always alone,

you come flying without shadow or name,
without candy, or mouth, or roses
you come flying

And there he appeared, lickety-split, hovering over the temple, balancing on its needle, atop a tower, a simple anti-gravity trick, young again, a complete makeover, radiating transfiguration.

Sadly, blinking made him disappear even though Larice had strained to keep her eyes open and record every detail as if she had turned into her Leica camera. Not a trace. Poof! Gone to the astral realm hiding behind layers of illusion. Her photo memory failing, she tried repeating the poem, stressing the phrase, *you come,* so loudly she transformed into a harpy screaming at the Mormon church.

Where did you go? Her voice cracked. The silent response turned her shouts into a long wail, a cry shattering her eardrums. Not a single light came on in any of the homes by the temple as she continued to weep strong heaves with each blast of tears. She lost complete control as moans radiated from her gut, waves of torment, cresting in a piercing cacophony of shrieks.

Exhausted after thirty minutes of runaway convulsions, she gulped and stopped, wondering if she had slipped into another dimension. She might even be locked in some pre-rapture transit point or stuck on some midway path between hell and the Mount of Transfiguration. How come no one heard her?

Grief can unhinge a person. She had read about the case of a mother identifying her dead child in the county morgue only to drop over and join her daughter on the cold table. What was it that Rosemarie said about the magnet? Why stick around and wail?

Such thoughts obsessed Larice so thoroughly she didn't notice that a young girl in a fluffy yellow taffeta dress was sitting next to her on the concrete ledge by the front steps.

"I've been seeing him for two months," she said. "This is his favorite spot to hover. Do you know he married my grandmother in this Mormon church? I bet you didn't know that."

The girl was quite beautiful with yellow strands of ribbon and tiny glittery bows woven in her braids. Her face was moon shaped with eyes that tended to wander as if she were looking through you to something coming.

"I love it when he dances. He doesn't always. Sometimes he just drifts and his wings get cloudy and limp. But when he's dancing, he lights up and I feel like I could fly too. Is this the first time for you?"

Dizzy from her crying, Larice felt like her head was about to pop. She patted her face and lightly touched her left shoulder to make sure she was still alive. She looked at her watch to gauge how long she had been crying and turned to the girl.

When Larice had left the shopping mall parking lot, she had begun to reconsider plan B. She still had her gun locked away in her glove compartment, but the gun seemed to be pointing more at her than the cop. The fast track to her lover did seem to be through death's door. His granddaughter showing up right after her vision and its ensuing cry-marathon didn't seem quite fair. How much could she take?

"What are you doing up so late at night? What are you, ten years old?" She plopped down on the grass and went limp, afraid to say another word since her throat hurt so much. Staring at the girl, Larice opened wide her startled eyes and blurted out, "I know you. You're that girl from McDonald's. I saw you do a cartwheel."

"I'm eleven, not ten. Maybe I'm that girl. Maybe not. All you need to know is that I keep track of him."

Mazie told Larice that she was mentally twenty-five years old. She'd heard about Larice from her aunties. Everybody on the rez knew about her, the white woman in love with VE, overwhelmed with grief. She figured Larice would show up sooner or later and had been keeping a vigil to catch her. She had a message from her aunties who would have talked with Larice directly, but they shied away from talking about the dead. Her mother couldn't help Larice because she was drunk with sorrow ever since she tried to kneel down next to her father's body, covered in blood, and the police pushed her back and secured the crime scene, keeping it that way for days while the FBI gathered evidence. Her mother didn't have a chance to say what needed to be said or sing what needed to be sung. No one in the tribe could touch the hoop dancer's body.

"So you see, he had to come back."

Mazie said more while looking up at the pinnacle tower, her arms flopping at her side as she stretched on her tiptoes.

"No more tonight. Maybe tomorrow."

The message from Mazie's aunties to Larice was simple. It wasn't a message at all. It was a request. "Follow the tears."

Mazie explained that her mother thought Larice was crying for everyone that missed her father. Her mother's cries were inaudible and without tears. The sorrow she carried around had almost broken her since she had to add it to the loss of her great-great-grandparents during the 1877 war with the U.S. Army, the loss of her beloved great-uncle during the Korean War who always kept track of the Nez Perce spirits walking around downtown Lewiston, and the death of her uncle whose car went off Highway 12 and into the Clearwater River where he sat entrapped until he drowned, plus the fact that so many other male relatives had died young because of the tears they also carried that they tried to dry with alcohol.

Even before the whites first arrived, her mother told her that the ancestors were grieving the horrific deaths in their family from strange diseases that left their faces pock marked and twisted in grief. Some ancestors had laments that they sang to the Snake River, songs that the current carried west to the Columbia River and the Pacific Ocean. Her mother had no more tear ducts and her mouth could not wail or sob like the old ones. The sorrow was choking her. It was good that Larice wailed and that she could hear her cries from blocks away, clear to the allotment land where her family lived, twenty-one miles away.

:: THIRTY-ONE ::

The wind shook the parched shrubs lining the concrete walk-way and whirled around the needle on top of the temple tower. The church hissed and shook as dark clouds rushed overhead like fists searching for a fight. Instead of the scent of rain, a strong smell of tobacco and stale beer came from the direction of the dark homes across the street. Larice thought she saw a figure walk-ing toward them, but it was only a crumpled newspaper stuck on a tree by her car. She glanced anxiously at the swaying pinnacle while Mazie slept soundly against her side. The church seemed angry at their presence and Larice stroked Mazie's head to wake her up. They needed to move and find safety from the storm. The sky was darkening green, sending whirligigs of dried leaves up and down the sidewalk.

The young girl wouldn't budge and Larice knew she wasn't strong enough to lift and carry her to the car. She had wrapped an old picnic blanket around them and started to unfold it, gently waking the girl, when a van raced across the parking lot and came to a screeching halt at the back entrance of the temple.

Instantly, she drew the girl closer to her and froze. Should she shake Mazie awake and make a dash for her car? Whoever was in the van looked agitated and frantic. Best to sit still for a few minutes and wait. Pretty soon, she heard weird sounds coming from the roof but she dared not step away from the front steps and look up. Someone, probably the man from the van, was up there screaming. Larice realized she had to act fast. Struggling with Mazie, she shook her awake. The girl was in the midst of a dream. "I can't find him," she kept saying as if Larice was there in her dream helping her.

"Quick. Mazie."

Before they were on their feet, a skinny man with a jerky shuffle ran across the lawn and barked at them, his voice hoarse and crackly. They couldn't understand a word he was saying. When they didn't respond, he stared at them, then started shouting again. What he said was blotted out by a whistling sound coming from inside the church and up on the roof. Panicked, he looked back at where he had come from, his left leg dragging like a dead stick. The wind blew his pants out, making him look like a scarecrow with gray hair sticking straight out from his head. He hesitated for a second, then grabbed Mazie's hand and pulled her away from Larice who grabbed her back so hard she nearly fell down.

"Let her go, you old coot. Don't you touch her."

The wind howled harder, pelting them with rain. Larice regained her balance, seized Mazie in her arms and ran toward the car. The man looked confused, then furious. Something held him back from chasing them. He looked up at the roof, straining to see or hear something.

He's crazy, thought Larice.

No more than ten feet away from them, his stick body stretched up on its tip toes, froze and stared at the roof. Suddenly, with what seemed like super human effort, he dragged his broken body back across the side lawn and retreated inside the back door of the church.

Mazie was wide awake, watching the man. She didn't seem afraid or even concerned, only intent on following his every move. Larice started the engine, and Mazie's hand grabbed the keys, twisted them and pulled them out of the ignition.

Larice tried to get the keys. The girl hid them behind her back. The kid meant business. She explained that they couldn't leave. There was something she had to do. She insisted that she had something she needed to ask that man.

"That horrible man?" Larice was beside herself. There was no way she was going back to that temple. "I'd rather go to hell."

"Then I'm not going to tell you where I live."

Mazie tried to get out of the car, but her dress got entangled with the wet blanket, and she wasn't fast enough to escape Larice who had grabbed the edge of her skirt in a death grip. After negotiating for twenty minutes with lots of *no ways* and *yes ways* and an assortment of threats that neither Larice nor Mazie had any intention of making good, they came to a truce. Mazie would get exactly two minutes to ask her question, but Larice must be present. Non-negotiable. Larice wasn't used to children, especially ones that claimed to be mentally twenty-five and assumed the stance of a reasoning adult. As a result, she failed miserably to understand what was at stake and simply caved in when faced with no alternative.

Larice was falling into another dimension, but not the one she expected, not the dark slide to death's door or the wild ride of revenge. When Mazie was stretching on her tiptoes to see if her grandfather was hovering over the temple, Larice realized she would do anything for this child whose perfect balance could only be a direct gift from the hoop dancer who chose to appear to the eleven-year-old whenever he needed or wanted. Why he appeared at the Mormon temple was a complete mystery to Larice, but something had brought them together on this miserable night to share a split second of transcendence. If that skinny old man was the night janitor, Eddie, then there was even more reason to stay close to Mazie, face the old coot, and then return the child home.

As fast as they came, the storm clouds were racing due east toward the Nez Perce reservation, crossing over Mann Lake and Webb Ridge to sprinkle rain on Sweetwater and Lapwai, going as far as Kooskia and Kamiah, where a monster's heart with coyote magic and a little blood helped to create the people who have lived on these lands for 130 centuries and were still walking the creek banks and canyons, working in the banks and grocery stores, studying how to help the coho salmon that morphs from glittery silver to iridescent red survive in ferocious splendor, watching the lamprey eels dance in the streams, and sitting in stillness to hear the cry of wolves and howls of hope.

With trepidation, the older woman walked the young girl around the temple trying to find a window to peek inside. Her years as a photographer made her a believer in reconnaissance. But there were no windows only a massive brick wall that made the building seem more like a mausoleum or a vault. They scouted the back and found a plain brown door that looked like a service entrance. They knocked, soft at first and then harder and harder until they were pounding with four fists and laughing because they felt silly standing there in the middle of the night trying to talk with what must be only a crabby old man.

Mazie stepped back and started singing a song her grandmother taught her about a butterfly that won't leave its cocoon. *Fly away, fly away blue wings.* She raised her arms and twirled, letting her yellow dress spin, making a pattern of flickering lights across the back dimly-lite steps. She almost seemed happy when the door opened.

A crumbled face stared out.

"This girl needs to ask you a question," snapped Larice, keeping a distance between herself and the ugly man.

"Who the hell are you?" he asked glaring at Larice. "Leave the Nez Perce brat and go." Quickly, he opened the door wider. Larice grabbed Mazie and backed away.

"I have a gun," she responded. "Don't you dare touch her." It was a ridiculous statement since the gun was still tucked away in her glove compartment.

The man laughed. He leaned from the doorway, his stick leg safe inside, his shoulders stretching, his right hand almost reaching them. Larice couldn't tell if he was trying to grab Mazie again, this time to pull her inside. Something about him seemed completely distorted, the parts of his face freezing, then disappearing, and his left eye didn't seem to work at all.

"Ask him," urged Larice, wondering if they should run.

"Why do you give him food?" questioned the girl as if nothing was amiss, her words ending in a soft, floating *ooo*, practically a musical note.

The man swung his leg outside the door and shook his entire body. "Damn you," he screamed.

As he lunged, trying to grab hold of the girl, they turned and ran as fast as they could, back across the wet grass, around the bushes, and straight down the front concrete pathway to the car. Larice glanced back and could see that he was following them, skipping and hopping, his stick leg holding him back just enough so they were able to get in the car, lock the doors, and speed off.

Larice felt her heart was going to explode. She could sense her chest tighten then burst into a searing pain. Shaking, Mazie was holding her hand, her eyes filled with tears.

:: THIRTY-TWO ::

The cozy bedroom looked out on a grove of trees rimming a creek bed, a feast of late summer yellow, coyote and whiplash willows clutching the sandy soil, stubby bush-trees with dense branches, hiding finches and swallows. The walls were decorated with bead bags, strings of necklaces, old violins, a guitar, and a pale deerskin dress, with five layers of lazy stitch black and white beads in bold bent stripes, making it seem as if the dress had a pair of wings from the chest across the shoulders and down along the arms. Larice was covered in a well-worn star quilt, and an old TV sat at the foot of the bed, piled high with dusty videos, books, and magazines. She could hear someone humming in the house. When she tried to sit up, her muscles refused.

"You shouldn't mess with spirits," said the short, stocky woman who came in with a tray of coffee and warm biscuits.

"Where am I?" Larice was surprised by her worried voice.

"Safe. My sister spent hours talking with our grandniece. You are lucky. Old man Harris heard the crash. He stays up late. Can't sleep. He knows Mazie. Brought you and her right here. Lucky. The car still works after you plowed into that fire hydrant. Rest. You can't mess with hungry spirits unless you are strong." The woman smiled with her eyes and sat down next to her on the bed when Mazie burst into the room and gave Larice the warmest hug she had ever felt. It made her dizzy.

"Auntie says you had a fright, but your heart is strong." Mazie's eyes sparkled brown flecks of gold as she looked into

Larice's face, scanning for signs of pain. She hugged her again and slid off the quilt, announcing she was going to get her other auntie.

The woman called Vel explained that her sister, Gracie, wanted to talk with her about the temple. Their family was Mormon from way back when Brigham Young instructed his followers to travel the Salmon and Snake Rivers into Nez Perce country. No one in her family believed anymore the legends of the Nephites or their stories about the Lamanites. The Mormons were searching in vain for her ancestors. The DNA would prove nothing. It was probably that Shoshone guy that one of her great-grannies fell for that got them to go to temple in the first place. They never went anymore or to Sunday brunch at their neighbor's homes to hear about the blessings of the priesthood. Out of respect, they kept the *Book of Mormon* and the *Old and New Testaments* in the living room while continuing their research on world religions, having read the tracts of Catholics, Presbyterians, Methodists, Baptists, Assembly of God, Nazarenes, and what she called migrating faiths, circulating their spirit words in car part businesses, garages, abandoned store fronts, and hotel banquet halls. She showed Larice the latest bulletin from *Blessed Hope* about listening to prophets and staying pure for the rapture. Lately, she and her sister were reading the Koran, using the Abdullah Yusuf Ali transliteration because they loved looking at the Arabic script; even though they couldn't read it, it gave a feeling they were closer to the spirit of the passages. They were thinking about buying another translation by Muhammad Taqi al-Din al-Hilali and Muhammad Muhsin Khan since the words were slippery and the footnotes brought up many questions.

"Those desert religions, they were onto something." Vel told her about her young days hitchhiking down to New Mexico and Arizona, staying with the Acoma and Hopi. "They believe in fierce laws and ordinances. Nez Perce would rather roam. Find out about the world. Every spring Gracie and I head over to Seattle for the opening game of the Mariner's. Have you been to Safeco field?"

Larice interrupted Vel to ask where their home was located and discovered the sisters had a modest home past Burrell Avenue on a deadend street a few miles from where she had her encounter with the fire hydrant.

Mazie walked slowly back in the bedroom, holding her auntie's hand. Gracie was at least ten years older than Vel. She could have been in her seventies or even eighties. Her hair was pure white and pulled back from her face in a twisted bun on her head. She was tall and a little stooped in her left shoulder as if a weight was attached. She tried to straighten when she sat down, steadying herself by placing her delicate fingers on the frayed quilt. Vel sat down on the opposite side of the bed while Mazie climbed up and curled next to Larice.

"So you are the grieving woman."

Larice felt embarrassed. Did every Nez Perce on and off the reservation know about her? Barbs was right. She shouldn't have called the tribal headquarters so many times. Her pleadings to Cass couldn't have helped either. At least Mazie's mother wasn't bothered by her endless sorrow.

"I saw him," Larice said hesitantly.

"We know. We only thought Mazie had seen him. The girl told us about you and about the janitor in the temple."

The sisters tried to persuade Larice to stay with them for a few days. Weird things were happening in the river valley. A small child had fallen into the Clearwater and disappeared. A man was knifed at Mann Lake. The trees in Hells Canyon were brittle. Fire was certain to come. Best to stay close to home for a few days and not tempt the spirits.

Larice tried to explain that she didn't believe in spirits, but she believed in what she saw on top of the Mormon temple.

"She has a restless heart," Gracie told Vel.

"He had a restless heart," Vel responded.

"Can I meet Mazie's grandmother or mother?" Larice asked.

Mazie giggled and moved closer to her auntie Vel. The two sisters looked at each other, stood up and asked Mazie to come with them. They were gone for at least forty minutes, giving Larice the chance to go back over the stormy night at the temple. She was determined to return and see if her beloved would reappear. Mazie would come with her. Together, they could stay in her car with lots of Subway sandwiches, bottles of water and juice, and clean blankets with fluffy pillows. And let's not forget the gun for protection in case that janitor returned. What fun. A stakeout. A vision stakeout. The Nez Perce still encourage some young people to seek their *weyekin* or spirit being, a rock, plant, animal or even a water molecule to guide them. Mazie might even go on one in a year or two. Or maybe her family didn't believe in them anymore. She would have to check it out with the aunties, that's for certain. They were going to be tough since she didn't think they trusted her.

"We want you to watch something." Gracie came back into the bedroom without her sister or Mazie. She pulled out an old VHS from the bottom of the stack and pushed it into the player underneath the TV. The video showed a middle-aged woman dancing slowly in a large circle. Her steps were soft and deliberate. Close to her young girls in jingle dresses whirled.

"That's Mazie's grandmother, almost thirty years ago. She died seven years before her ex-husband, your lover, was shot."

Larice watched a fragile woman in a beautiful red dress with white buckskin boots in a one-two drumbeat take small steps propelling her in suspended inches along the dance circle close to young girls in colorful fringed shawls and jingle dresses whirling. She was a still point in the midst of spirals. The video refocused on the fragile woman coming closer until only her upper body and face filled the frame that shifted into a kaleidoscope woman of rainbow hues and blurring, multiplying profiles.

"Her mother needs more time. She left yesterday for Mukilteo to live with her cousins, close to the water. She has taken the right step, to leave until her sadness can become a strength. Grief cannot be hurried."

Gracie explained that Mazie was a gift. With her visions came danger.

She cautioned Larice not to return to the temple. Spirits played games. It was too dangerous for her or the girl. In the old days, the temple would have helped the dead find passage to the next world. The Mormons used to believe in seer stones and the vision world. But they let their material success harden their beliefs. Today they hid inside temples that were more like tombs with fancy furniture and chandeliers, inventing silly secrets, and forgetting the sacred groves and the celestial sky.

"It's the pawnshop you need to visit," Gracie added. "There you might find some answers from the man with the rope."

:: THIRTY-THREE ::

Her life seemed like one long, ill-planned, over-wrought wild goose chase. Those honkers who flew low over the Clearwater waking up campers knew where they were going, so why didn't she? Why was she fated never to know the end game or even the basics about where she was going? In arrow formation, the feathery migrators skimmed the river while Larice was flailing up and down 21st, driving with a bent front bumper and busted headlight. Thank God it's dark, she thought. Any cop stopping her would face the worst juju since Plan B was still in the glove compartment. She didn't know how she would react. She'd already spent two years raving about curses with secret plans of annihilation interrupted by random sensations of guilt. No doubt, she was unhinged. In Mazie she saw her lover's grace. She knew warmth once again. She wanted to hold onto the child that wasn't hers. She wanted to punish the man who killed her beloved. She couldn't make anything right.

Larice would have to face her demons alone. She was glad Mazie was safe with her aunties. They were tough. Grief hadn't broken them. She could see it in the way Gracie walked into the bedroom, deliberate steps, no rushing, no flailing, a million reasons to get angry, break down, drink yourself to death, tear apart your house, your car, your appliances, even the electrical wiring, but something inside recalibrates and finds a way to stay walking upright in beauty, see the ravishing greed and walk right through the fire wall, the shit storm, the maelstrom of hate, and keep walking, showing your children and grandchildren a way to move, your soul intact.

The pawnshop at the top of the hill looked completely deserted. Not a single light inside or out, not even the street lamps on either side of the highway. Blackout.

She started to open the car door when she heard a voice whisper, "Don't approach from the front."

Underneath a grass-stained blanket in the back, Mazie emerged with a cautious glance.

"Jesus," shouted Larice. "Your aunts are going to kill you and then kill me."

Mazie ignored her, urging a strategy of reconnaissance and reminding Larice about the binoculars that were underneath the gun in her glove compartment.

"You don't miss a thing," said Larice.

Mazie covered up her mouth and pointed out the window. Larice crouched down and then took a chance and peeped, watching the shadow of a man rushing toward the pawnshop. Ever so slowly, Larice flipped open the glove compartment and groped for the binoculars. She didn't need much light to see that the man was dragging his left leg. They stayed perfectly still as they waited to see what he would do. First, he went up to the front door and banged hard, and then he went to the barred windows, grabbed them and started to yank. He worked his way along the windows, pulling and pushing with no luck, then disappeared around the corner of the building. They could hear clatter and what sounded like garbage cans falling over.

Her eyes glued to the binoculars, Larice scanned the building for the twisted shape. She almost shrieked when the face of the man from the Mormon Temple popped into her sight. He had reappeared from the north side of the building. He seemed to be glaring at her, his eyes bulging and enraged. He couldn't possibly see her, she thought. They were parked far enough away in the darkness. What was he looking for? Then she noticed the old, white Volvo parked on the side of the pawnshop. The man limped over to his car, got out a crowbar and hobbled to the Volvo, swinging the metal rod in his right arm. When he got close, he swung it down with all his might against the driver's side window. Nothing happened. He started swinging harder until the glass shattered.

Larice watched as he ransacked the car, throwing onto the grass two sleeping bags, five boxes of books, a dozen bottles of apple juice, an enormous plastic bag of potato chips, and what looked like cleaning products.

In the midst of his trashing the car, he looked up and cowered. What at first seemed like a light had come on inside the Pawnshop. But it wasn't a light. Larice sniffed. It could be fire. But it wasn't fire.

Almost against his will, the man limped up the walkway, but before he reached the front door he heard something and ran around the back of the building. The lights inside continued to glow for a few seconds before the building once again went dark.

"He's inside," whispered Mazie. "The homeless man."

"Shush," Larice hissed. She was trying to figure out if she was hallucinating. Had she seen the man from the Mormon Temple? Suppose she had seen something else, and that something else made her pull Mazie to her.

"You don't have to go inside," said Mazie, holding Larice's hand and leaning her head against the older woman's shoulder.

"I'm afraid." Larice didn't want to get out of the car. Why couldn't they just sit inside, catch their breath, then drive away and cut themselves off from what happened two years ago? So what if the man with the rope knew something about the cop's face when he shot her beloved? So what if the crooked man had seen her lover's astral projection hover over the Mormon Temple? So what if she had? It could be a hallucination, pure and simple. Let the man with the rope spend the rest of his life trying to make sense of what happened two years ago. Why did the cop shoot? Who's to blame? Who benefited? Who gets to keep shooting?

Larice wanted to stay inside the car with Mazie. That was suddenly enough.

"Me too," responded Mazie.

"You too what?" asked Larice.

"Afraid."

"Let's leave." Larice started the engine and was about the pull away when Mazie opened the passenger door and jumped out. In a flash she was running toward the pawnshop, running like a young antelope, slender legs gliding above the pavement, suspended, until she reached the front door that suddenly opened and shut behind her.

"Mazie," Larice screamed, charging after the girl.

She pounded on the dirty brown door until the sides of her hands ached and turned black and blue. No one answered. Panicking, she considered driving back to the aunties' home, but was afraid to move from the door. Mazie was inside and she was outside. She couldn't call the police. She was frozen in Lewiston. There was no one she could turn to, not her sister, not the entire congregation of Mount Zion Baptist, not her friends at the newspaper, not even that lawyer of impossible cases. She, alone, would have to figure out a way to get inside and rescue Mazie. The longer the girl was gone the harder it would be for Larice to be effective. She remembered seeing a TV show that said it was in the first five minutes that you could thwart a kidnapping. It was already twenty minutes. But this wasn't a kidnapping. Mazie had voluntarily run inside the pawnshop. And that same pawnshop was ignoring her pounding pleas to get inside.

Desperate times call for desperate measures. She headed back to her car, opened the glove compartment and pulled out Plan B.

PART FOUR

EDDIE

:: THIRTY-FOUR ::

Parking lots all the way if he slipped through the broken fence behind Discount Vacuum, took a straight line from US Marine Corps Recruiting to First Interstate Pawn, then a crisp diagonal between Cannon Material and Cash & Carry with a hop across the intersection of G and 19th to at last Jack where Cindy started at seven am, late for him, but perfect for her. Red glow. Trudge, trudge. Cindy was his queen. She smiled, picture perfect, her corporate copy gray shirt, black slacks, and black shoes, no questions asked, and knew to hand him premium roast. Up all night in the cool blue-white glow, welcoming the jolt to de-digitalize. Only coffee and Cindy until Fred walked in with his FFL problems.

"I don't fuckin' want to give them my address. You fuckin' have to have an address to fill in this fuckin' form." Freddie fouled out. No Federal Firearms License without an address.

He needed more time with Cindy to watch her rhythm of order and serve, her thick blonde hair pulled back under a wispy net, no deterrent to sheer adoration. Fred was a fly, buzzing. Eddie had on his best jeans and denim jacket, felt the spring in his legs from the walk with his book tucked inside his jacket that was taken out and placed carefully on the table next to premium roast until Fred made him move the book aside when he plopped down his extreme sausage and mini pancakes. Fred needled him as usual about his reading. Eddie sat back, calm like a rider, the smooth bass voice of Sam Elliot whispering inside his head about the purple sage where horses melted into dark-blue night, a million stars wheeling overhead. He loved smiling at Cindy. Cindy was his queen. And with his coffee too hot, he slid the bent paperback into his jacket and drifted until Fred interrupted again.

"They want a number." Fred crumpled the form and pretended to eat it.

"Lie."

Fred started repeating the same two words, "No way" tagged with a curt laugh halfway between a grunt and a snide. He continued to make fun of Eddie and his paper westerns. "You don't need a horse, Eddie. You need a good smartphone. A GPS to get you home." Unlike Eddie and his pressed jeans and Goodwill jackets, Fred preferred a worn, button-down Oxford yellow shirt and creased khakis. Fred's wife insisted he not lapse into retirement wear. No sweats outside the house. No sandals with socks. No end-of-days sweatshirts.

Eddie preferred living alone. No family pests or prying neighbors. Only Cindy, weekday mornings at seven am. Life was good, like the slogan said. He had a wide-open loft above a converted auto parts store at the edge of the industrial park, as the Chamber liked to call the rundown section of town. He didn't even have a proper address, but he had plenty of electricity. Eddie was pleased with how he lived. He knew a lot about Cindy, how many parking fines she had, how her sixteen-year-old boy was doing community service, picking up trash at the Locomotive Park across Main Street, how she once got evicted from the Lewis-Clark Trailer Park, how she was a member of Mount Zion Baptist and why she wanted the administrative assistant job that was opening at the church. The fat manager at Jack had eyes for her if you could call them eyes, more like dough balls above chunky pink cheeks and cascading neck folds, a waddle dawdler who rolled around in the kitchen calling her *super sweet* with his high-pitched squeaky voice. No man for her. Eddie didn't want a wife or even a girlfriend. But the fat manager wasn't going to have her. He had a better chance of ending up as lard for the fries or shot dead like that evil Mormon bishop in *Riders* who gets justice from a pair of blazing black guns.

He knew a few things about Fred, too, how he talked about guns, bragging about his big collection stored in his basement rec room when Eddie knew his wife wouldn't let him even have a snake gun. Fred insured anything worth anything in his home, and Eddie knew that there wasn't a dime for any gun collection that supposedly included a 1917 mint-condition Colt 1911, a WWII era 7.65 Walther PP, an Erfurt 9mm Luger, or a Browning Superposed Centennial 12ga/30.06 shotgun. The closest Fred would get to that shotgun would be hearing the word Browning spoken by his Mormon brethren. He'd heard a lot of shop talk about guns at the temple and how the elder Jonathan Browning, not his genius gun-designer son, John Moses, would engrave his guns with the words, "Holiness to the Lord—Our Preservation," a clever advertising slogan if there ever was one. No, Fred didn't have an antique gun collection. Fred had no guns. But Fred had gotten him his temporary janitor job at the LDS meetinghouse to fill in for the facilities manager who was about to be shunned. Eddie checked doors, four nights a week because of recent vandalism, plenty time left for midnight free riding and hoofing it over to Jack by seven am, M-F.

"What about using your address?" asked Fred.

"What would I want an FFL for?"

"I'm thinking about selling my collection to this guy in California. Could be a bunch of money in it for me. Time is right. I could sign over my guns to you and you could bring them down to Sacramento for me. I give you $200 for the FFL fee and $500 for the trip plus expenses, like gas, motel, food."

"Don't they want fingerprints?" Eddie asked, watching how far Fred would go with his deception. How would he get out of his mountain of lies?

Fred looked at him and guffawed into his iced caramel. "Got you, didn't I? I'd never sell my gun collection for anything. It's what I'm giving my son. It's his inheritance. But your finger-prints are plastered over the FBI database, aren't they? Come on. Say it."

Eddie didn't even wince. No pity either. Fred was a Mor-mon case study, transfixed by crime, not the angel Moroni or the prophecies of Joseph Smith. He was slumming with Eddie, living on the dark side at Jack. Curious and cold, he observed Fred, like a scientist examining a fuzzy white rabbit before dissection. The rabbit would never catch on. That's why it was at the bottom of the food chain, a continual supply for predators.

Eddie looked past him toward the order counter. Cindy was out of sight in the back, behind the grill and the aluminum vents. He could hear her multitasking since Debbie Downer, the once-more-out-of-retirement lady whose arthritis made her lean on the counter while taking orders with heaving breaths, hadn't showed up to share the fast food playbook. That was rough on Cindy but good for him since he hated watching the old wom-an limp from counter to tabletop to booth, wiping off crumbs with bright blue plastic gloves two sizes too large for her shrinking hands. Premium roast didn't quite taste the same if you couldn't watch Cindy, so he decided to dump Fred, cut short his morning indulgence and walk to the Locomotive Park. Check on Cindy's son. Maybe strike up a conversation. Procure an inside track. He could always climb up on the steam engine and find a wasp-free seat and read again, for the eighth time, how Lassiter got the gal and bagged the Mormons. Eddie had stolen twenty-eight Zane Greys and keep reading them in cycles. The books were friends that he kept in a single bookcase underneath his bedroom window away from the screen wall. The screen was his life, but he knew the difference between pixels and riding the cañons and the purple sage. He wasn't a loser addict or pathetic cyber bully. He wanted the rabbits. He wanted the believers who think their words match their guts. Blow up their stupid, fucking truth.

The net wasn't the piñon and juniper forests of southern Utah, but it was still a call to adventure with blazing black guns, crashing boulders, lioness women, and dark-browed villains. No heroes allowed.

:: THIRTY-FIVE ::

Tenmile Canyon past Homestead to Short, then hide in the bushes and search. Nobody to bother him with ATVs. Load up the pictures from Google, sit back, and try to ignore everything around him, especially the posters of Jack working out on stair steps or with his film crew making a documentary, probably about Jack and how he managed to make millions of crappy hamburgers that conjured up power lunches. Eddie believed that once every place on earth is uploaded digitally its material form would vanish, no more polluting stink bugs, toxic streams, clogging dams, oil barges, mutant wheat elevators, green backpackers, greener mountain bikers, camo-faced hunters, camouflaged survivalists, wasting deer, gangster crows or Jacks. Deleted. Then the real war that humans lusted after could begin. Not a war over oil or water or food but a war of image, music, text, a true, glorious internet war. Obliteration. Apocalyptic death. Gutted minds.

He usually didn't travel with his iPad but the thought of sighting Cindy made him forget his aching body and night of cleaning the meetinghouse side rooms followed by the prep work for the new roof, and bring along a guaranteed time-waster to gaa-gaa his sweetheart. No one messed with the guy with the latest iPad. He could sit for hours at Jack.

Too cheap to hire professionals, his Mormon boss instructed him last night to start pulling off torn composite and flashing. He threw the blue tarp at him like he was a life-form not worth saving once the final days arrived. Eddie had sat on the edge of the roof and cursed the stars and the Mormon god, then made a mental note of taking down the church website. Let them spread their lies in the face of my wrath, he thought. With every rip, he imagined digital death.

The smell of summer through his open windows cheered him, and he hesitated for a second over how these brief forays into deluded hope would soon be gone. Better to walk while you can and watch Cindy. Small comforts in the face of doom.

The sprinklers at Jack sprayed a fine mist filled with rainbows as the rising sun over the Lewiston hills backlit the fast food oasis. The gray, grit hills behind the restaurant made the green verdant grass along the sidewalk look neon electric. The strips around Jack, geometric and narrow, prickled with sparkling light from the rising sun reflected through the irrigated water. Geese honked over the river, competing with traffic buzz from the highway, a perfect morning to snatch a glimpse of Cindy.

A large "Now Hiring" sign disturbed his odd seven am equilibrium. And, sure enough, Cindy was gone. In her place was the old lady who had aged another five years overnight. Her hips betrayed her body as she waddled from behind the order counter to fill the condiment bins, spilling little cups of half-and-half on the tile floor. Eddie bent over and picked them up, tossing them in the narrow bin and palming a dozen packets of barbeque dipping sauce in front of her eyes. She didn't say a word. No *thank you*. No *put it back*. She just made her painful way back to the counter where two young Hispanic guys waited, one hunched over and shy, the other stiff and defiant, eager for her to make a mistake so he could unload on her about some crap on his mind. At least Cindy wasn't there to smile at these guys. Her one failing: she was forced to be nice to every customer at Jack, company policy, and she seemed to enjoy it though she might scream at home. He was undecided.

Google maps comforted him.

Those busy crowd sourcers uploading street views, interiors, roof shots, 3D, go-pro drones, family photos around the living room table, bedroom peeks, want the earth to evaporate. Eddie could feel the surge of millions shooting digital nirvana.

Tenmile Canyon stayed green, no winter shots, a place without cars, no animals, only green trees that blur into brown earth if you get too close. Best to stay above the canyon trail winding along the ridges that steepen then slide into walls slipping down to the river. Snake shapes crawling underneath the slanted lines of plowed wheat, fading to red brown. Headphones dripping in irony. Steely Dan pumping out his tune about that other Jack and that wheel turning around until it falls into Google space, stuck. Eddie was eager for the satellite updates and thought about a dirt bike with a thousand clicking cameras to sort and send. But he hated Google and its button-down British lawyers with their community guidelines or lie lines. Unworthy. Rural Idaho was nowhere to them, not like Bond Street in London or Sana'a in Yemen. Yeah for bomb craters and shoppers. What they have in common are blurred faces, no identities on the dead and about to be dead. How soon, Eddie wondered, before the dead can be identified both above and below the earth?

Random thoughts amuse.

The two brown guys hopped in their pickup and drove up the hill toward the Orchards that are no longer there. Absent apricot, peach, and pear.

Jack was quiet. Not even a drive-through order. Eddie thought about how great it would be if everyone was eviscerated. He knew the Mormons had their own sophisticated satellite systems that would work even if the USA went down in a big electronic ditch. He admired their resourcefulness. Don't just stockpile toilet paper, food and water. The tabernacle choir singing in front of Mount Rushmore, South Dakota, transmitted through a private cluster of orbiting workstations 23,300 miles above the equator, super linked to Europe. What a beginning. The Saints were linked throughout the planet earth and into space, the words of the chosen Prophet radiating intimate, encoded messages about the apocalypse. Internet capabilities layered into transmitters with the sovereignty of the Mormon god. That was omniscient vision with a clear understanding of the apocalyptic nature of global communications systems, hurried along by the speed of digital uploads by crowds of workers, shoppers, and bombers.

Flashing news: After rapid searching on social media, Cindy was working at the rival McDonald's a few blocks away. If he hurried, he could recon about her hours or maybe luck out and find her smiling face beneath a cute black baseball hat, a form fitting T, much more athletic and fashionable for the young generation if there were young people working in the hangout of the Nez Perce who for some reason loved this stopping place with its sticky pancakes. Hispanics were taking over Jack, the Nez Perce were hogging the tables at McDonald's, and he was afraid to go into Wendy, ha, ha, watch out for those STDs. Eddie was happy. Cindy was back.

A few surreptitious snaps saved for his eyes only. Upload someone else's bitch. No, Cindy was saved in all the meanings of the word. Save, savior, savor, savory. To deliver from peril or hurt. To defend. To make secure. To avoid a fall. To prevent. To keep and cherish until death do us part. To relish. To edify. To appetize. Take it and taste.

The grass was already dry as a bone from the mid-morning heat as Eddie cut across to Locomotive Park where he dodged the city's white pickup making rounds to flush out any homeless sleeping under the Camas Prairie Railroad #92 with its pea green caboose and its glorious bygone days of cutting deep across the rez, plowing up the Nez Perce root supply, and sending the Indians running to McDonald's where they could watch on their cellphones *Wild Wild West* filmed with 1955 decommissioned Camas

Prairie railroad cars and brought back for the pure purpose of Hollywood gone mad on steampunk technology and never-ending westerns.

The city worker gave Eddie the mean eye, squatted down to glance under the engine, cars, and caboose, and sped away in under three minutes. Another American work day finished as Eddie laughed at the pathetic threat, kept his focus on the golden arches, and steered himself to the last living remnant of hope for mankind, Cindy.

:: THIRTY-SIX ::

Specks of white sugar stuck to his right cheek, humming Eddie improvised lyrics to a lazy rap: *Snack on libertar for lunch. Call out virus from hell to munch.* He hated the boy scouts of the internet, those avengers for individual freedom and liberation from government constraint. He dreamed of infecting their computers with malware that branched and twisted each time the word *freedom* appeared on their websites, blogs, emails, texts, and twitters, wherever they were communicating, transmitting, or distributing their stupidity. Criminals were technolusters, early adopters, not poster boys with cute grins and firm handshakes. Libertarians didn't understand that the word *utopia* meant no place. With their breezy love of future techno wonders, the heroes of the dark net were just more little white rabbits looking in mirrors with startled eyes, catching only their own reflection and missing the infinite fragments of their individuo waiting for the gun blast. Techno Horror, now that's a concept Eddie embraced. Techno Death. Techno Armageddon. If you could not feel in your gut the first time you turned on a computer the pure force of evil, then you were merely an ad slave blinded by false promises of status and power or a crunchy libertarian flying into *Eddie's Mouth*. That's what he called his five screens radiating a blue Kool-Aid glow. *Eddie's Mouth. Come to my mouth. Come to me. Come to me.*

With his computer, he could shred true confessions, hoax the hoaxers, and blow up the *tremendous positive effect technology can have on our world,* especially the drivel streaming from YouTube lips and Google brains.

He preferred to think he was *born to die,* three words he'd lifted from the Palestinians who understood the liberation of threat and explosives even though he thought the Middle East was a cesspool of such depth not even the god of Abraham in his merciless manifestations could untangle that Gordian knot. He loved piling on metaphors until their direction collapsed under their weight or was it the velocity of intent or was it simply stopped (since how can direction collapse?) by some slimy cypercop recently graduated from Singularity University? Then again gravitational forces do distort space/time so horrendously that direction could be said to collapse at the event horizon of a black hole, hence a singularity, not a peculiarity, but a final force that matters. Ha, ha.

Life is good.

For the last twenty-four hours he had alternated between reading blogs of patriotic white-out men and equally anti-government libertarian fools. Their anger and righteousness tickled him pink but after acute boredom set in, he realized that they weren't even worth taunting or lickety-splitting, a new technique he was honing to create fatal encounters. Merging their websites into a 3D mosaic might provide him with hours of fascinating code manufacturing. But was it worth his time? He needed something meatier.

Real crime was always more fun since everyone had an opinion, usually based on their inner parrot inherited from mom and dad that they liked *sharing.* Local crime was even better since he could observe the interaction between newspapers, websites, YouTube channels, the men in blue wannabees, victims, perps, families of victims, families of perps, his neighbors, the guys at Jack, the Mormons who didn't know he was listening when he was hanging around in the basement or up on the roof, or the kids at Locomotive Park who smoked dope and had less hope in the world than he did. Then there were the cops and their co-horts in the injustice system, eager woman lawyers and judges, especially young ones under thirty-five. He had a special soft-ware for *lawyer spotting* targeted on three townie attorneys whose *sincerity* was detrimental to the world's future. Their client lists and confidential files sparked many a merry evening. Why would someone walk into the crosshairs?

So much to do. So little time.

Prioritize.

So much more fun to upload the state cop's dashcam onto his channel hellline community ++ and let the comments roll without restraints (unless you call those community lie guides restraint) kicked off into a shit storm of hatred and vengeance, stirred at precise moments with cruelty.

On one side the Indian lovers and sympathizers, on the other the Indian haters.

Another dead Nez Perce dissected online. Eddie checked ev-ery morning like clockwork, skimming the new comments, count-ing how many ragesults, and wondering still why the sad people who were losing their trust in humanity as they wrote kept coming back for more? How far could they be pushed before they pushed back? Would they try to find out who stands behind clever mon-ikers like *hellokitty, oogiesmuncher, allconsuminghate, toofakemelody, herolink, magicorca, superscrew, nanonymous, or armymadman*? Never, thought Ed-die. Little white rabbits. Too dumb to know they were going down the hole where the game is toxic slipping. Fake identity fawning, fun filtering, flamboyant flaming fuck. Too unstable to play the game? Then go shoot someone, then revolve to said identity and shoot again and again. Virtual brains. Can't take the perform and punch code of digital emptiness, a concept gleaned from Bud's isms attachment to groundlessness, the unconditioned condition of nonshapeshifting? Holy Bud.

The short, frail fifty-six-year-old Nez Perce guy heard the spirits chanting when he ignored the cop's polite request to exit the car. The aunt and uncle ghosts walking up the Cottonwood Creek hillside followed by cousins, nieces and nephews coming to greet him on the rez where he insisted he was safe and no fucking state cop could tell him to get out of the car since he was home and the state cop was an invader, an alien life form, that most remarkable of strangers, a white man. Hey, look, there's his father trudging, waiting for this poor sucker to receive like communion five shots for resistance eternal, the pathos Indian clutching the steering wheel and chanting to the cop so his spirit relatives could hear, *You are nothing but a white man.* Over and over the guy chanted, holding onto the car because he knew he was joining his family soon, his brother drowned in the Clearwater River, sitting in a car trapped because the drunk driver missed the curve and hurtled them down the hill into the fast, cold current where he contemplated the sacred river that rushed in his mouth, his cousin hanging from a prison cell because no one checked on a DUI depress-here-even-more until only a belted neck was a door, and his niece hit on the side of a road tipsying home blotto blotting out the face of her infant child. The jokey hoax. The skinny Nez Perce didn't see the great spirit lurking, the dashcam, the digital crime scene, played constantly online for meet-and-greet comments that ran hour after hour for Eddie and his millions on cellphones held while youtubers eat breakfast, shit, ride the subway, fracturing their likes and dislikes into numerical data scooped up for house cleaners, outdoor wear, and anti-aging creams. Fingertip death. Repeat death.

Too bad the dashcam missed the blow-apart gunshots and recorded only the sound. Missing were the entwined bodies of cop and Indian rolling down a slight incline where the pickup truck had stopped because there was nowhere to go on this dead end reservation road. Too bad we can't run it again in reverse like *Psy-*

cho and laugh even harder, the knife coming out and the splattered blood going back in the soft, white flesh. How much sympathy can you have for a crinkled, over the hill Nez Perce guy who can't get it together to open a door because this state cop isn't going to wait for the rez cops. He's in a hurry. He's got a live one. And live ones must obey or die.

Shot five times. You can hear the pops.

Imagine the action off-stage. Close is hearing the blast of death. Plenty of room for viewers to opinionate their brains on a new Indian war, or heroic (and polite) cop, or rabid viewer hoax. What cinematic bliss!!! Dashcam magic.

Tune in and babel for Eddie. Add your comments below. Smile for the camera.

:: THIRTY-SEVEN ::

No Cindy in sight. The McDonald's at the bottom of 21st was crowded by seven am with hassled moms dragging kids, underpaid office slaves eating cheap, the usual crowd of Nez Perce jawing over pancakes, and lone men devouring screens. Eddie did his usual pretend iPad routine, a series of peeks and sneaks at the customers and swift glances to the order counter, hoping that by some miracle of scheduling Cindy might appear since her teammate was barfing in the back, but only pimply faces smiling continued to take orders and fat women with attitude to scoop French fries. He flicked on a YouTube 1931 *Riders* and pictured Cindy on a palomino in a golden, sunlit world, her horse prancing in time with her bouncing blonde locks. Together they slipped into a maze of cañons to hide from the desperadoes hunting them, flinty Mormons with blood atonement minds and cruel deputies with Mormon masters. Frantically, they galloped to the sheltering darkness of stone cliffs. Two lovers hounded by blood spillers. Eddie liked Grey's cold definition of men: blood spillers. What else was there to add?

He looked up when two women walked in that he recognized from his lawyer spotting software, Cass Zinski and Flora Hendricks, so serious and intent with their cloth briefcases, comfy flats and black pencil skirts. Not quite librarians, but close. Too bad he couldn't overhear their conversation. He could only watch their mouths moving because, close by, two junior high kids were sneering at their screens and swearing in decibels, proving beyond a doubt they were total shitheads. Eddie speculated that the goody lawyers were talking about some unemployed mom who needed help breast feeding her soon-to-be loser baby while she searched for some shitting job they would find for her out of the kindness of their hearts. *Don't delay the inevitable*, he wanted to scream at them, out shouting the jhs punks. The women should be taking the baby and mom away and selling them in some other country that doesn't pretend it doesn't have slavery. Let them scrub the floors in Saudi Arabia. The only freedom left in AMERICA was outsourced long ago.

People started leaving the golden arches for their punish jobs and Eddie bored of the 1931 *Riders*. He switched to map questing and headed south of Tenmile Canyon to Lake Waha, over Craig Mountain towards the Salmon River country. If he had money, he'd live up China Creek or on the Oxbow where nobody would hassle him. He'd grow potatoes and fish for sockeye, build an earth shelter and hunt for deer. Life could be good. He'd look for the bones of Hime Payex and burn incense for Toohoolhoolzote, the only Nez Perce besides Looking Glass that counted, not that drunk Injun on YouTube dashcam chanting at the white cop. He deserved to die a thousand times a day with haters watching. Eddie glanced at the three Nez Perce left at the table five feet away, whining about fishing rights with their potbellies and mushy faces, fat trappers like their fat fuck neighbors. All rotting flesh. Probably relatives of the dashcam Indian who didn't know enough to carry a gun. Chants didn't help that fucker. He should have blasted the cop away and headed out across the rez. He was already at Cottonwood Creek. Shoot and run. What's wrong with these twenty-first century Nez Perce? Toss peacenik Chief Joseph away. Embrace Looking Glass and White Bird. Repeat after Toolhoolhoolzote: *I will never surrender to a deceitful white chief.* And die a hero at Bear Paw, not shot by some sniffling state cop making you bend to his school teacher command: *Get out of the car.* For what? Going through a stop sign? Going ten miles over the speed limit on a deserted county road on the rez? Drinking? You can't chant that cop away. One recourse. Blast the fucker. Rearm every Nez Perce and take back Toohoolhoolzote's land. Rise up my little red brothers and fight!

Eddie headed back north up the Snake River past the petroglyphs at Buffalo Eddy and made his way slowing to Tenmile Canyon and then Lewiston. His map questing strengthened his resolve to never let the dashcam stop playing. He scrolled through the morning's comments and imagined the hundreds of years ahead with fun-loving haters and troll pranksters spewing digital spit at the pathetic drunk, an Indian clown worthy of highlights online: *That cop is a fucking coward. He should have beat the living dog shit out of that Indian and not shot him. Tribal land is not foreign land. The cop had the right to pursue and shoot. Good job officer. Racist Indians. Drunken injun acting the fool. God bless this Trooper. This guy deserves what he got. Human debris. That's what this Indian is. I'd a shot this motherfucker long before the cop did. Pow Pow to his head. Justified shooting. Thank Mr. Policeman. Less trash on this earth. Damn Indians should never have alcohol. I would have shot him too. Gotta love a stupid Indian. Justifiable homicide. The officer did a great job. Cop of the year! Fucking native is a dum fuck! White police rule. The officer was polite calling him sir before he shot him. It's about time you natives learn you can't break the law and hide on your land. He did justice, nuff said. A drunk injun got what he deserved. I hope he died a slow painful death. LOLOLOLOLOLOLOL. This cop was waaaaaaay too good with him. A clean shoot. Just another white man...who's still alive!!!!! Justified!!!! Native Americans smell like shit. I am sick of people being sympathetic to a peckerwood who is obviously breaking the law. I would have pulled the trigger. He shot Big Chief Thunder!! I would shoot him in the fuckin face. I feel for the cop. WHITES WIN AGAIN WHOOOOOOO!!!!!*

Eddie disliked the overuse of exclamation points when a single cruel phrase would do, but he noted that the haters way outnumbered the soft hearts. Yes, a few counter-haters emerged with tough talk about the cop, but their numbers were insignificant.

The haters rule the internet. It's a fact of life. It is their desert where they are left to die or survive according to their spirit and strength, or was that what Grey said? Eddie was worried that Cindy wouldn't hold up under scrutiny. He thought about making a website about her and seeing what the reactions were. If she folded, he would know she was too weak for the future of America. The crucible of the internet made or broke people just like the sage lands of Cochise or the steep canyons of Toohoolhoolzote. Pain was necessary. Digital pain absolute.

Chief Joseph's words had ruined the Nez Perce. The differences between the bands had left only the weak behind. The cop was cleaning up the refuse.

Shutting off his iPad, he glanced out the window at the morning traffic speeding up and down 21st. A young girl around eleven-years-old was pointing across the street at a homeless bum leaning against the light pole. The guy had the funniest face, a pleading happy face, with a thick rope wrapped around his right arm. Eddie laughed out loud, too loud. The two women lawyers were already outside leaving the parking lot, but there were still a few stragglers who twisted their necks to see what was so funny. He quickly opened his iPad back up and pretended to turn it on. He watched as the girl pulled against her mother, a Nez Perce for sure with her dumpy black hair, fat legs, and soggy eyes, probably couldn't even get a job at Albertson's, not that they would hire an Injun. The girl spun around and stared at him through the window glass. She latched onto Eddie's face and bore a hole through him with her eyes, a life force that made him sit up straight and throw his head back. She wouldn't look away until her mother pulled her so hard she almost fell over.

One of the leftover Nez Perce got up and walked outside. They started talking with the mother, trying to calm her down.

Eddie used the distraction to close up shop, slip out the side door, head back to his apartment. He had no line of sight with the Nez Perce girl, and for now he wanted to keep it that way. He would have to do some reconnaissance about her and the mother. He had her license plate number. That was a start. And he'd picked up the license plate numbers of every NP who ate at the Mc that morning. He was also going to find out what that meeting was about between Zinski and Hendricks. He could never be too cautious.

:: THIRTY-EIGHT ::

Eddie believed he was an artist the equal of Zane Grey, an artist that wanted inside the human confusion to discharge thunderbolts, start electrical chain reactions and unstop the gridlock of daily life. Inside each artist was a secret troll wanting to do as much harm as possible. In league with the devil. Giving the devil his due. Unfortunately, readers were fickle flitterers, pumpers of power lines slinking through cable wires, no better than ego transformers bent on writing, not reading, unaware that no one is listening even when everyone can hear. Drivel overload.

If digital equals consciousness, then dig down deep, dwarf divers. No more fluster bluster from school teachers and grammarians, if they still exist or have disappeared into the emerging ice age. Base your lie-life on the never-ending morality play of dashcam's likes and dislikes. Go in the night to wink and nod at vani-video fair. Here's his new conundrum. How long can the comments accumulate in metadata clouds before some cooling block in arid Washington State experienced total electronic meltdown? It was only a hypothetical. But it did make him think about exponentially futile gestures and the explosion of nothing. In practice, Eddie's main challenge was to stir the dashcam at the right moments and hope someone who really cared about that piece of shit Nez Perce would tune in to protest. Wasn't there anyone out there who knew this guy? Most supporters were cleverly sympathetic as if they were asked to have an opinion for a survey at their office. He particularly hated pathetic advice to the cop:

I don't know the circumstances, but I kept thinking just back away
a bit and leave the guy in the truck. Keep him talking and call for
help. Really doesn't seem necessary to shoot him.

Or, even worse:

I don't agree with the actions of either party on this one...both
were in the wrong.

Eddie hated that more than anything. Neutrality. Both are
good. Both are bad. And spit on pro/con gibberish: the hiding
place of talking heads for news shows (prime, cable, digital or
hybridized, racing across social media and fluttering fingertips)
along with English 101 slave instructors. Where was the queen of
hearts when the world needed her?

Time to intervene he thought. Stir the pot. How about this
salvo to get them to rise and fight:

Since you have little academic knowledge and understanding of
demographics, you can only misperceive what you see. It is com-
mon for an uneducated fool to cheer state-sanctioned violence.

That will bring them out swinging. Troll the trolls. Eddie had
a basketful of techniques to keep the swell exciting, laundry lists
of nasty business to insert, catalogued under topics such as crotch
insults, cunt shots, three word take-downs, two-word take-downs,
death ray expletives. Eddie loved his taunting guise of invented
liberal replies (so easy to imitate):

You become confused as to the context of my comment. I was re-
sponding to another comment that was stretching an assumption.
I am sure you probably become confused quiet often and reading/
writing is probably not your thing. You do come from an inferior
class and don't know it.

Let all hell break lose. Class warfare is not as colorful as race hatred, he had to admit, but the results were the same. You are fucked.

Spread the ease/disease of the artist wandering the dashcam
of a tragico-pathetico shooting that takes place in the front yard
of a Nez Perce shaman who believes in friendship and peace. An-

other fucking Chief Joseph descendant. You little dead Nez Perce man. That tribal elder didn't help you, did he? That cop shot you dead in front of the old man's grandkids, crouched in the kitchen, afraid to look outside at the swirling lights. Did the kiddies hear the last chant of their relative? Was anyone drumming?

> *your just another white guy your just another white guy your just another white guy your just another white guy your just another white guy your just another white guy your just another white guy your just another white guy your just another white guy your just another white guy your just another white guy your just another white guy!!!!!!!!!!!!!!!!!!!!!!!!!!!!!!!!!!!!!LOLOLOLOLOLOL-OLOLOLOLOLOLOLOLOLOLOLOLOLOL*

See what happens to words in real time? Eddie watched as the final sounds of the soon to be dead Injun played back in mock comments as if anyone in this fucking world would have a drop of sympathy or should he say a nanodrop of sympathy for some fool shot by a cop? Let the game continue:

> *I am educated in more ways than you know you illiterate socio-path. That is an unprovoked attempted head shot by the officer and an execution in the later stages.*

Countered by:

> *You're a real fucking winner dude. At no point in this dashcam does anyone get executed, in fact this cop likely saved HIMSELF from being executed.*

Boring. Eddie was starting to drift away and where would his reader/writers go? He cherished the intimacy of insult. He began to see troubling patterns of repeated abuse so redundant as to make his channel watchers yawn in disgust. His dashcam might be reaching its dreaded end-of-midnight conclusion. He'd have to find another dashcam joy ride. Worse, somebody in cybersympathy was blocking the juiciest tidbits from his loyal fan base. Tonight some duperhero took the time to cut and paste into Google lielines a truly juicy comment:

Kill them all. Every fuckin injun. Finish the job we started in 1877.

That reference to the war of 1877 between the Wallowa band of the Nez Perce and the U.S. Army headed by the one-armed praying general, O.O. Howard, was the first piece of fact mentioned in any of the 5,789 pages of comments and still printing he had come across. He wondered if the date had made the comment viler, prompting the labor intensive effort of having it blocked from his channel. Eddie would have to check into the reality effect of dates on the human psyche. Gravestones had dates. There might be something to references of lived life as the philosophers liked to call it, especially those living ones writing about digital culture who had fallen prey to false dichotomies. They should read Dante's *Inferno* and leave the philosophizing to Eddie, who besides reading Zane Grey and western Americana obsessively, got a hard-on for Gramsci, Butler, Žižek and that strange man, Alain Badiou. When he was feeling itchy, Eddie tuned into MOCs online offered by the Institute for Strategy & Competitiveness at Harvard and Goldsmiths at University of London. Why not slurp philosophy, especially with its obsession about power? The best minds were gathering online, blogging their hearts and slinging mud like their fellow neonaz and bornagainandagain. Eddie's dashcam was a handy playing field to test out his ideas. Academics should embrace the vile and follow him to the empire of fools even though the Nez Perce cop shooting spectacle might be drawing to a close. Ah, well, you have to stay alert to survive. *Go back, Jack, and do it again.*

Lest anyone think it was all fun, Eddie did spend a few hours checking on the Nez Perce girl and her dowdy mommie from the golden arches. Rehab for the mom. No surprise there. Most days and nights, the girl lived with great-aunties, still holding onto a tiny speck of allotment land. After this morning's display on 21st, the mom was probably sitting in some pale green office examining her fingernails. Probably didn't even care about her kid.

And, bingo, the real shocker even for Eddie, the kid used to have a grandfather. The one and only shot-dead Nez Perce. What are the odds? Actually, Eddie tried to figure out the odds. They were somewhere around one in 12,000,000, given the demographics of Lewiston and the Nez Perce reservation.

He'd wait on what Zinski and Hendricks were talking about in their meeting since the lead about the Nez Perce kid, Mazie, had opened up an entirely new playfield. He had plenty of research ahead to discover whether she was a descendant of that old, peace-lover Chief Joseph or his personal favorite, Toolhoolhoolzote. Maybe he could tweak her hatred into an act worthy of a dashcam channel. The crucible of the digital desert made a man into a man, the ritual of pain, that's what Eddie searched for in the dark hours of night.

:: THIRTY-NINE ::

Their mouths were moving but he couldn't make out their words even after plowing through a lipreading course on You-Tube. He had covertly videoed their conversation at the Mc with his FREDI P2P from Sears, just in case he could reconstruct some tidbit to help his search through the office files of the two women lawyers. Next time he'd buy a better recorder pen. His was a piece of shit. He strained his neck scanning their mouths in slow-mo. All he needed was one word to save hours of labor. The video was almost useless since side angles captured only emphatic words, like *evict*. He nailed that one coming out of the mouth of Hendricks, the public defender. And since that was her bread and butter in this town, it was little help. He played their talk backwards and forwards, fast and slow. Eddie concluded it was like watching some exotic female ritual dating back to the days of *Ardipithecus ramidus*, four million years ago. Eddie fixated on the pair. Tipping their heads ever so slightly toward each other, the two women nodded like primitive dolls, their chins rising for momentary reflection, their heads shaking for signs of truth or lie, their eyes blinking at pregnant pauses, and their hands lifted in proto friend/foe gestures. Eddie discovered hours later the conversation was about a homeless man, named Sheldon Deacon. He quickly learned that the guy had a bench warrant in force.

That was interesting, but not very. It was more fun to keep watching the two women. He considered uploading the conversation to a website about white women terrorists that he was constructing. What joy to produce the voice overs. He wasn't much interested in people without homes. Who the fuck had a home, anyway? Everyone he knew was running or trying to escape home. What good were those compassionate crime courts meant to address the urgent needs of losers? They only ended up spewing out druggies and mental cases that didn't show up for their weekly roundup and public humiliation before a weary judge and a peanut gallery filled with more druggies, mental cases, legal interns, police guards, and noisy commoners. March through the social machine at your own risk and emerge a perfectly formed citizen who knows how to shower and sleep in a bed. In prison, at least, they got tough or died, hardened to the power pressing their necks to the ground and ready to pick up their computers and hack the hell out of America. Maximum-security-prison-tempered coders, what a godsend, raw talent that Eddie dreamed about accessing and would have if he wasn't such a true believer in complete isolation from the dangers of computer talk between humans.

He was able to access the security camera outside the Mc and prove beyond a doubt that as the two women lawyers were leaving, they had seen the push-pull between Mazie and her drunken mom. Neither stopped. They hesitated but did not stop. Why was that? Curious. With his facial recognition software, he couldn't make out who the sillyface man across the street was that Mazie was pointing at. Maybe another drunk relative. It was a laugh. A Nez Perce drama across the tide of traffic on 21st. Why not? It used to be their homeland a blink of an eye ago.

What made Eddie suddenly twitch was watching the frozen girl staring into the window at what he knew was himself. She even looked up at the video camera on the outside of the building and back into the restaurant as if she knew what he would be doing later that evening. And guess what? That was exactly what he was doing sixteen hours later. Watching her watching him. Defiant little Injun. Was she a time jumper? She definitely knew him and what he was going to do, but how could she? He couldn't decipher the how. He played it back more times than the conversation between the women lawyers. The girl would stare in the window, then stare up at the video camera. She slowly and deliberately sequenced the stares. No lip reading necessary. She wanted him to know that she was watching him. That was simply impossible, thought Eddie. She didn't even have a cellphone on her little girl person, no email account, no text account, no cyber life. Off the grid. A low rider. She could be dangerous.

Eddie tried tracing her back through what he had on file about the Chief Joseph clone, William Allyn, whose front yard on the rez was where Mazie's grandfather was shot dead. Maybe there was some hocus-pocus still floating around in the tribe. He'd heard rumors that a recent version of the dreamer religion encouraged flying around in a trance, bringing back news of the spirit world to sorry-eyed Nez Perce in dead-end jobs, and dictating dance steps during first foods feasts. Sadly enough, sniff-sniff, their dreamer trips seemed more like a New Age happy-happy-tan rendezvous without booze than a hard-core visit to the dead. Those day dozers on the rez could never have kept up with Toolhoolhoolzote on his spotted black pony riding into Montana where he stood his ground and practiced his tough dreamer religion that seized red power not dancing directions. Eddie sensed that Mazie might be like Lozen, a prophetess of the Chihenne Chiricahua Apache, whose special power could detect which direction the white brute cavalry was charging from. No make-me-feel-better crap. Only straight up find-the-fuckers-first. Lozen's Apache god, Ussen, gave her the uncanny ability to locate the enemy. No satellite surveillance. No high-tech optical drones. Simply stand up, stretch your arms out, and feel the pulse positioning. That beats flying to find dance steps every time. Standing in front of the Mc window, staring into Eddie's eyes in real time and through his sophisticated video equipment, Mazie radiated power. She had found her enemy.

Maybe she could discover where he lived with her power. And why was she pointing at that homeless idiot, unless the homeless idiot was connected somehow to what the girl was planning to do? From the tape, it looked like the kid wanted to go back across the street and talk with the homeless guy. Her mother was the one stopping her from crossing.

Watching the tape again, Eddie noticed that the bum's rope wound around his arm and waist with a tail hanging down his left leg, touching the sidewalk. A rope guy. Maybe he's going to hang himself with it, he thought. Then he remembered the one word that the two women lawyers seemed to be saying that didn't make any sense. He thought it must be dope. But it wasn't. It was rope. Rope. Rope. God damn. This was the homeless guy they were looking for, right across the street from the two women. How ridiculous. The girl knew. And she knew that he would figure it out too. But those two women lawyers didn't have a clue.

Eddie quickly scanned through other street surveillance tapes of that day and evening. The rope guy had disappeared from 21st. No online camera seemed to know where this Sheldon guy was. The problem with homeless people is that they were paranoid and low tech. A troubling combination. Some weren't, of course, and had patched together low shelf phones and pads to stay connected. But some, some very few, were completely unwired and leery of the surveillance state. The cops should implant those doggie ID chips in them or subcutaneous transponders like torture scientists put in turtles, birds, lions, elephants, and crocodiles.

He did know from driving to his night janitor job at the Mormon church that homeless people liked to skirt, skitter and skittle the edges of parking lots at the mall and the litter-filled ravine up 21st to Thain. Eddie might have to drive and look. Or he could first check with the guy at Subway who liked to distribute food at night to the vagrants wandering around the garbage bins.

Work both ends, thought Eddie. He liked the idea that he was looking for the same person that Cass Zinski was looking for, a competition that he knew he could win. And if he could find the rope guy, he knew it would lead him straight to Mazie and to finding out why she was using her power against him. Was her stare a taunt or a challenge? Maybe she saw his dashcam or one of her great-aunties saw it or her dopey mom saw it or somebody in that long line of Nez Perce cousins, nephews, nieces and crowd sources had pushed hard to block his YouTube channel. Maybe finally he would locate someone who gave a damn about that lame seeker and drooling chanter, her grandfather. Enemies were always curious about each other. They gave life meaning.

:: FORTY ::

Buzzsaw in the head. Eddie hankered to see Cindy, but her hours at Mc overlapped with his night gig at the Mormon meeting house/church/temple/gathering place/picnic area. He had to re-sign himself to vi-spotting through the security cameras, mainly gawking at the top of her black baseball cap with a stray blonde hair rising to the ventilation duct. Eddie was beginning to think that Cindy was a low-return investment, and he was convinced she couldn't hold out under net scrutiny. He'd set a few die-hard Chinese netizens onto her Facebook drivel in hopes of scoring pornwords and spitbanter, but she folded fast. Very disappoint-ing. She saw no artistry in the troll and didn't understand how the altego functioned. Positive points for converting to PGP, even though pretty good privacy was not good enough. He might have to shelve Cindy until he caught his homeless man and solved the puzzle of Mazie. The blonde didn't look like she was going any-where fast.

On his way to the eleven pm hand-over at work, Eddie had driven up 21st checking the parking lots for the rope guy. He'd even stopped in for a subterranean sandwich to pump the Asian manager who knew numbers and cleaning products better than Subway food. His response was evasive, almost secretive. He must have seen the rope guy or why act like he didn't know what Eddie was talking about? Eddie was good at interrogation tech-niques. He shifted the conversation into parallel and waited for the odd detail that didn't belong. Two oddities popped up: the need for an emergency shelter during a babbling talk about the new housing development along the Snake River and the dangers in the ravine up the hill when they were chatting about changes in landscape design. Conclusion: the rope guy was on the loose and the manager was fretting about how the idiot might get hurt or trapped in the ravine. That was how Eddie interpreted the tense left jaw, pursed lips, and right ear rubbing of the immigrant employee facing his non-future in America. Sensing an opportunity, Eddie handed over to the manager a spare key he had for the Mormon church, telling the Subway worker in detail when and how to use it. He wrote down the times when Eddie knew the church was safe for someone to hide there without detection. He laid it out, pretending he was confiding in the manager about the problems with his night-janitor job and how he needed a back-up in case something happened to him or in case there was a person in crisis that needed a safe haven for a night. Eddie was always amazed at how people, especially the dazed crawlers fresh-off-the-boat, needed to think people cared. What was that about? Some evolutionary tic in *homo sapiens* that died out thousands of years ago, lingering as a genetic or kinetic memory? Or, maybe the flotsam of the globe needed a momentary stay in a quiet cesspool to catch their collective breath? The Chinese man carefully took the key, examined it for a few seconds, and slipped it in his shit-green front apron pocket then softly rested his right hand over the key above his skinny belly. Eddie didn't know whether to laugh or classify what had happened as an event. He rarely witnessed them.

The clock was ticking. Eddie had only around fifty minutes before he had to arrive at work. The roof repairs were in full swing and the picnic area needed another cleaning since the volunteer day crew yakked instead of scrubbed. How much could the LDS talk about the Prophet's words and gloat about courage? What kind of fucking courage does it take to stand against profanity? Try standing against a Barrett M107 and then let's talk. Like the Nez Perce, the Mormons were finished, their spiritual roots yanked out and set ablaze in the wastes of corporations and the CIA. On second thought, the Nez Perce could learn something from those Mormons on how to invest those casino profits. Try shopping malls.

He liked to imagine himself an internet entrepreneur. Why not a bath tub full of bullets as a special giveaway prize for the one millionth commentator on the "I'll play your death everyday" dashcam? Redundancy needed incentives. Insults needed rehabilitation. He had to attract new flash heroes and folk swatters to the Nez Perce shooting channel. People didn't realize how much work was behind the façade of unreality. Events happen forever. Events never happen. Swipe reality clean.

Such sweet thoughts on a starry-skied evening made Eddie almost teary eyed.

He pulled over into the empty parking lot at the edge of the ravine and parked, trying to decide if he was going to hoof it. Map questing offered nothing in real time, only useless updates, lagging years behind. Real time was a nasty nut to crack. No replay mode. No pan in, no pan out. He'd have to chance it since the sillyface man with the rope looked as harmless as Fred, his Jack buddy, nothing going on inside, except fantasy stuffing pilfered from years of watching TV. Just in case, he pulled out his .357 from the glove compartment, a sleek 2.5" beauty, and stuck it in his side holster. His insurance policy.

Hardly across the lot to the trail, he heard what he couldn't believe was Karen Carpenter's voice, singing *Sha la la*, and caught a glimpse of a white car hood under a drooping cottonwood tree at the back of Macy's. What the fuck?

Sure enough, wedged against the dirt bank was an old Mercury station wagon with a top rack loaded with broken crap, its side fake wood panels dented and peeling. A junk collector, thought

Eddie. He walked over and taped on the window, just in case the squatter might have some info about rope man.

No answer.

He knocked again and noticed a mound of bedding had moved away from him. He walked over to the other side and knocked harder. Strewn around the asphalt outside the passenger door was a bright red, broken tape of *Ticket to Ride* and a smattering of used taco sauce packets from KFC. A Carpenter groupie binging on fried chicken. He stood for a few seconds listening to *When I Was Young* until his stomach revolted and he banged against the car door with his foot.

A nasty head of gray hair emerged from the pile of blankets and comforters and stuck out her tongue at him.

Encouraged by her glare, Eddie opened the door and poked his head inside. She dove under the covers and started to whimper. Eddie laughed then looked around at the doll display inside.

"Love the crucifixion," he said, pulling out the Barbie swinging from the rearview mirror, and chucking it on the dirt.

The inside of the car smelled of newspapers, urine, and musty clothing. Another filthy, low-tech rider. Eddie was tempted to pull the covers away and get a good look, but he decided the human wreck might know something.

"I've got money," he said. "Money for information."

"How much?" he heard a reed voice whisper.

"Plenty."

Straining, the woman braced herself against the busted seats and stared at him. She wasn't as old as he imagined. Maybe only fifty. And not that wasted. She knew what was what. Yes, on seeing the man with the rope. Yes, on a list of others that Eddie didn't care about like sneaky boys, sneakier cops, circus clowns, and a parade of animals. Something was going on in that ravine. She'd seen strange lights and heard a growling noise that penetrated the car's floor mats.

Eddie kept feeding her five-dollar bills while she rambled on about dancing girls and old women. The man with the rope, or maybe it was a man without a rope, definitely went in, but she didn't know if he came out. None of them seemed to come out. No one.

She turned up the cassette tape when Karen began to croon, *Close to you*, and drifted away until Eddie waved another fiver in her face. He'd seen this before. Addicted to old songs by long dead singers. If she wasn't so low tech, she'd probably be binging on YouTube Karen, posting comments about how it used to be wonderful and blabbing on about her angel voice. The bitch starved herself to death. Dah!!! Hoax the hoaxers!!!!

:: FORTY-ONE ::

Cold pockets of air collected along the north slope of the ravine, stroking Eddie's face as he made his way deeper into the maze of brush. He felt young again like his LRRP days in Vietnam, humping through the jungle alone. Loved that fantasy. No night vision goggles, only his wits and his sense of smell to defend against an enemy attack. Homeless people stunk in klicks. They could be a camp nearby within scent. He hopped over a small boulder and spun around, slicing both his arms to ward off predators. He laughed, stifling the sound with his hand. A war movie. He would have loved to act in a war movie or even a war which he'd heard was just like a war movie. He was having a cinema-psychic event without the blue glow of the screen. He avoided watching Vietnam flicks, especially *Full Metal Jacket* and *Apocalypse Now* that pathetic Fred could lip sync, and thought they were over priced sacks of existential bullshit about violence (Is it a war movie? Is it an anti-war movie?). Tonight he felt like killing some living thing in real time. Maybe a homeless guy. Cold air was a testy charge. Get the blood running. A blood-spiller. ZG would approve.

Then he heard the stick snap. He wasn't alone. Exhilarating.

Eddie might be in his late 50s, but he prided himself on his fitness, working with weights and Tae Kwon Do routines he learned in an earlier YouTube obsession. He skipped rope and had a freestanding punching bag, not a Bob Dummy that stares and doesn't say a thing when you smash it in the face. He even hooked up a cross training rope from the ceiling. Stay ahead of the curve. You never know what's around the corner.

He slowed his pace and listened. A snap again, but this time to the east. Whatever was moving out there might be circling around. Probably a drooling deer looking for a handout.

"Screw you," he shouted toward a looming cottonwood tree that shook in the rising wind.

Eddie kicked up a bunch of leaves and kept moving south into the ravine and away from the sound of traffic. Across an incline and a dried-up creek bed, he stopped beside a large boulder with trash scattered at its base.

Fuckin' LZ for vagrants. He waved his flashlight over the camping site and along the top of the huge rock. No one. He rummaged around the discarded cans and flipped over with his boot toe a playing card, the three of spades. Attaching his flashlight to his front belt, he bent down and poked at a shiny object that caught his eye, a small spoon, partly covered with *Twix* wrappers. Could be a trick to throw him off. He slowly picked it up, making sure there were no attached wires, and rubbed the handle between his fingers. Possibly sterling. He put it in his hip pocket and continued to walk around the deserted camp.

It was then he noticed legs dangling from the top of the boulder. They were swinging. Eddie didn't say a word. He stared hard wondering how somebody got up there. Must be a way up on the east side he hadn't noticed. The shoes were oddly familiar but he couldn't see enough of the torso to identify the wearer. Maybe size eight. Old gray white Nike Sky Highs, no shoelaces, a dangling sole.

"How the fuck did you get up there?" he yelled, craning his neck to see what he could without his flashlight. The darkness made it impossible to get even a vague sense of the upper body. Eddie detached his flashlight from his belt and swung the intense light over the rock.

Nothing. Whatever was there was gone.

"I get it. Playing games. I can play games, too."

Cold air caressed the back of his neck, and he spun around to see a retreating figure walking briskly away about ten yards farther south along the trail. When he waved his flashlight along the trail, he glimpsed a short, sinewy man steadily walking. No rope. Definitely no rope. He hadn't seen the guy's face, but he knew it wasn't silly-face, way too athletic. The rope guy waddled. This guy was smooth.

"Hey, you. I'm talking to you," Eddie shouted. "Asshole."

The guy was probably taking off because he shouldn't be there, thought Eddie. Maybe the guy thought he was a cop or vigilante on a drive-out-the-scum mission. Eddie started to walk faster. He was determined to catch up to the guy and find out if he knew rope man. He could feel the weight of his revolver against his back belt. Life was good.

He hoofed another one hundred yards downhill without luck. There seemed to be only one main trail both in and out of the ravine, and the dirt path was still heading down and by now Eddie figured it should have been heading uphill toward Preston with its careening lines of pickups and cop cars. He stopped and bent down to check the trail. The soil felt slimy. And he only then realized that he was surrounded in silence. Not a bird or bug sound. When he first stepped into the ravine, a nasty crow squawked and the bushes buzzed. Maybe he had hiked into a toxic dump where nothing grew. Slime only.

He went a few yards more and checked his watch. He'd been in the ravine four hours. That was impossible. He'd only walked possibly a mile. Four hours to walk a mile going downhill? But it had to be true because he saw the slightest glimmer of light from behind Lewiston hills on the east horizon. In another hour, the night sky would fade.

Then he saw the man again. This time behind him. Some-how he had circled around him. No stick clicks. No warning. Just there. Like he was waiting for him.

Eddie didn't like the game anymore. He shouted at him and gave him a litany of abuse. He unloaded and it felt good. *God damn homeless piece of shit!*

Then darkness came again without warning, and cold wrapped him in a cocoon.

To an orange sunrise, Eddie woke tired, so bone tired he wanted to fall back to sleep again and sleep for a thousand years, but he knew in his gut he'd better get out of that ravine as fast as he could. He retraced his steps and started to run, flinging his arms at his side, scraping against a tall stand of dry thistles, and tripping over the tangled roots of burnt sagebrush. Tossed on the ground hard, he could feel his left hip crunch. He pulled himself on his side and then yanked his right leg under him, pushing against the dirt with all his might to stand up. He tried to walk only to tumble back down. He struggled again to get on his feet. His left leg felt like it was detached. Finally upright, he swung the bum leg around with the full force of his upper body, letting his heavy left boot thud against the dirt. Slowly, he limped back to his car, each step sending pain waves up his hip into his lower back. He cursed so hard that foam was collecting at the corners of his mouth.

In a final effort, he scrambled up the bank to the parking lot of the shopping mall. The doll lady's car was gone. He only saw a delivery truck offloading behind Macy's.

Luckily, he still had his car keys. But when he dug them out of his pocket, he realized his flashlight and gun were gone. He must have dropped them in the ravine when he fell down. Too much pain. He wasn't using his head. Awkwardly, he managed to get in his car and close the door, locking it shut as if somebody was after him. But he knew there was nobody there.

The silence in his head hurt. Something was terribly wrong.

Even his hands ached as he tried to turn the key in the ignition. His fingernails were filthy like he had been digging in the earth. He dropped his hands away from the keys and stared at his fingers. They were more like claws. The skin was raw and caked in filth.

For the first time in his life, Eddie wanted to cry, but he couldn't. He sat in the parking lot in his car dry heaving, his throat a raspy tunnel of burning air.

:: FORTY-TWO ::

The ritual of pain wasn't as much fun as Eddie had imagined from his readings about Apache girls and boys who looked with contempt at their bloodied legs and broken arms, so he sucked away on a sweet perc-a-pop as he climbed the stairs, dragging his left leg up each step to the roof of the Mormon church. He needed air, billowing waves of cold air, to wake him up. Danger lurked in sleep that was pulling him under its choking chemical blanket. He hadn't bothered to keep track of how many pops he'd already had and worried their drowsiness would overtake him. His skin felt red hot and a rash had erupted over his face that he wanted to scratch, but his fingers were still raw from the twenty minutes of scrubbing in the basement bathroom to get off the layers of dirt under his fingernails. Must have been some panic reaction in the ravine when he was out cold. Maybe he had crawled or tried to dig a trench to hide from his pursuer. He couldn't remember. He stared at his hands that looked emaciated and bent, their knuckles swollen, the skin torn into tiny flaps. More troubling, his right leg felt like a stick when he rubbed his hand on his thigh to get the circulation moving. His muscle mass seemed to be melting.

He was beginning to feel his body was a tool manipulated by a stealth enemy intent on his destruction, and to ward off the attack he patted the stash of opioid lollipops in his back pocket. The pops would get him through the siege until he could figure out what was happening, maybe a virus he caught poking around the homeless camp or something that phantom guy did who wouldn't turn around so he could see his face, then circled and waited for him, half hidden behind a tree stump. Eddie shivered. He knew that guy from somewhere.

The two giant blue spruces at the north end of the roof banged their branches against the electrical wires that snaked near him. The night was ferocious. Cautiously, Eddie grasped the railing around the roof walkway and took several deep breaths. The air didn't seem to help and only made him feel dizzier. He hesitated, not certain if he should stay on the roof or go down. He didn't know what to do. Was his body locking up? His joints seemed frozen. He tried to turn his head. No luck. His neck was completely rigid. He could only stare, straight ahead, past the roof. The picnic tables at the end of the parking lot looked like they were hiding figures crouching in the dark grass. The spruces bashed against the roof, sending a tremor down his spine. Eddie almost tipped over. Under the groan of the wind he heard a soft voice calling.

What the fuck, he yelled as if to push the voice away.

The same mumbled words were repeated, this time closer. He still couldn't make out what they meant and yelled again, taunting the voice. *You think you can scare me? Fuck you.*

The wind suddenly died down, and after a few minutes of playing out several scenarios in his mind, Eddie made his way back to the rooftop door. He felt calmer.

Maybe it was that Ativan he popped to stop the shakes interfacing with his beloved lollipops that was creating this strange brew in the brain. Nobody was on the church grounds and who the hell would be talking to him up on the roof? Fear can paralyze the mind, he said to himself. *Nobody messes with my mind but me,* he chanted out loud, trying to laugh at his predicament, if it was a predicament, probably a passing setback, before he caught that fucker in the ravine and showed him what happens when you mess with the Eddie.

He surveyed the roof again, looking across the large parking lot that rimmed the church. Nothing. The two hundred-plus spaces were swept completely clean like no one had ever parked there or left behind a trace of human debris. The black asphalt expanse with its neat striped boxes seemed more like a holding area for a reunion of the scattered tribes of Israel, a favorite Mormon fantasy. Eddie chuckled to himself. I'm not crazy, he thought. The fuckin' world is crazy. The parking lot was probably built as an end of times LZ, big enough for some celestial spaceship to land.

Eddie was definitely feeling better. He made his way back down the stairs to the ground floor and limped outside, checking each window and ledge. Reconnaissance had replaced fear. Gather intel. Gather intel. The dark shadows from the parking lot lights might give cover so Eddie trudged to the far bushes and walked the boundary line. Too bad the church hadn't installed a perimeter warning system. Who cares about breaking and entering? You had to get the bastards as soon as they stepped foot on your property. Eddie stood for a while looking back at the church and the roof. He realized the distance was too great for the strange sounds he heard up on the roof. It was like someone was whispering in his ear. Intimate. Must have been those electrical lines. In storms, they can pick up the sounds of radio stations.

Life was good.

Popping another perc, Eddie sat at the edge of a picnic table and stretched out his tired legs. Only one hour left of work and he could drive home and get some rest. Nothing had turned out as he wanted so far. No man with the rope. No Mazie. His life seemed to have divided into two halves: before and after the ravine. No matter. He would fix it. Maybe use his GoPro to make a found documentary set at that homeless hiding place sort of like *Blair Witch Project*, but instead of witches, there would be these vampire vagrants, the best hoax ever to feed his new YouTube channel. He might even convince Fred to bump around in the dark with lots of distorted close-ups of his face. He'd have to get creative with enacting ritual sacrifice in the woods since even snuff movies were yawners online. Maybe the sacrifice could be a promise of future sacrifices, a chain email sacridoodle, urging viewers to choose a beloved pet or friend or family member to put to the test. Abraham and Isaac for the electronic masses. The idea had potential. What did he need a dead Nez Perce for anyway? The dashcam had played itself out in real time. Let that entire NP family rot their guts out at McDonald's, especially that mini-Lozen with her time jumping eyes. A new post-ravine day for Eddie. On to Hollywood, he said to his imaginary Fred as he puffed out his chest and stood up.

Even without looking, Eddie felt the guy in the ravine was back. Lifting his head, he saw the shoes again, the same dirty Nike Sky Highs, dancing above the thin needle tower on top of the church, two glowing white dots. The shoes were enveloped in some kind of antigravity force field, Eddie thought, or maybe he had popped an Ativan by mistake while contemplating his movie career. The rest of the body was hard to make out, except for a glittery hoop that descended along an emerging arm. Making an abrupt stop, the hoop spun off the arm and whizzed into the sky, sending off sparks like a Fourth of July firecracker. Then another hoop joined in and another, twirling and merging into wings and spheres that danced above the church.

Sitting back down, he watched as the hoops flew around like magic Frisbees, gradually returning to the man with the shoes. Gyrating circles covered his arms and legs, hundreds of hoops spinning as they careened up the torso, ascending up the neck and head until tens of thousands of hoops spun around the figure suspended over the temple. Only the man's face was shrouded by long black hair that drifted over the dancer's legs, straight hair so long it rose in tempo with the spinning hoops.

As if he was drawn to a magnet, Eddie walked toward the dancing man and stood by the large front door of the church, looking straight up at the apparition hovering over the temple tower.

In a puff of wind, the face appeared; a young man with deep-set eyes, a high forelock and feather-braided hair gazed down.

I think I know you, whispered Eddie.

:: FORTY-THREE ::

A circle of red ceramic bowls filled with oatmeal, squash soup, and corn grits surrounded the base of the needle tower, rising from the roof of the Mormon church. Four eagle feathers were attached to a pole with a red ribbon, resting against the tower, a nice touch for the no-age-but-new-agers. The Nez Perce loved red since it brought back the days of suffering in the 1877 war with the one-armed Christian general jawing on about farming while shooting women and children first, including those assimilators who were planting gardens and raising cattle. What else could you expect in a battle over land? *Kill them all* was still a popular comment on his dashcam site, the words reverberating for almost 140 years into the digital universe to repeat exponentially throughout the perched minds of a million likers. Direct contact with reader/writer/destroyers satisfied like reality never would.

Eddie had taken thousands of photos of the roof top and had spent all night Photoshop-layering the bowl images, ripping off as much as he could from food websites, Pinterest and cloudland. A masterpiece, his moving collage was almost ready to upload on his new YouTube channel. If that tiny time jumper was out there she would respond. He was having some problems with animating her grandfather's photo that he had found archived online at the *Lawrence Journal-World* when he won a hoop dancer contest at a dusty Kansas pow wow back in the 1980s. Eddie's hallucination the night before, a drug-bending of his mind, inspired psychedelic rainbows in the digital night sky and swirling oval eyes he had lifted off a cougar night vision sight. Maybe he had pursued the wrong calling. Could art rise above the hoax or the hoax-hoaxers? Perhaps.

One lesson he had learned: Never trust experience. The nights on the roof and in the ravine proved once again that reality was overrated, the stuff of slime. Better to draw out Mazie online than enter a maze of unpredictable occurrences, random incidents, and unreliable perceptions. The out-there simply didn't work. Further proof: his puzzle body was shedding muscle mass as each hour ticked by even when it was locked and loaded with an assortment of dark web drugs. Matter dissolved. So what. Eddie's digimind grew and morphed, entwining minute finger gestures with instathoughts, a violinist of the haunted house. No spectre or spook with dirty Nike Sky Highs could best his online creations.

Replaying the dashcam, he had frozen the exact moment the state cop had dragged VE out of his laughable mini pickup and examined the soon-to-be dead Nez Perce's shoes. Eddie figured he must have seen this detail of dirty white sneakers a million times but not registered it until the moment he dissected the dashcam in his attempt to identify the creep in the ravine. Either, the shoes were the same or someone had gone to the trouble to duplicate their effect, costuming a VE look alike, or the drugs had simply seized his mind and reprojected this dashcam image onto his experience to heighten the confusing impressions of *reality*.

He could have a digienemy lurking about who had the intelligence to understand the game; unlikely, since even hacktivists clung to old-fashioned ideas of morality or nihilism. In the end, they were mainly lib/rad/progress wimps trying to right the wrongs *in the world*. If he did have a digienemy in the world, he or miraculously she would live in Caracas, Aleppo, or St. Louis. Eddie called his potent/ial enemy rend-the-veil. What a joy.

Tweaking his Houdini software, Eddie reworked the shoes, trying to get the tips to bob and point toward the viewer. It was then he noticed out of the corner of his eye on an adjacent screen a small figure and the side of the roof template. He must have dragged some side debris into a layer without realizing it. Sometimes he worked so fast, his little fingers couldn't keep up the pace. He zoomed in and saw only the back of a small figure with its head peering over the side of the roof looking at something in the parking lot. Sure enough, there was another figure in the parking lot looking back up at the figure on the roof. Fatigue overtook Eddie. His mind was working so fast, trying to justify what he was seeing on the screen, that he let his world go dark. He went into sleep mode.

He sat down on the side of his bed and thought. One mistake? Yes. Two? No. Relational images could not be present without intent. But whose intent would it be?

The only conclusion: his computer was a biohazard. Level four. Complete anti-pathogen gear needed: positive pressure suites, circular containment tubes, APR doors, and a kick-ass decontamination system.

He should shut it down now before the inevitable nuke.

He couldn't.

The computer beckoned, a dark square monolith, floating about his metal slab desk, next to a row of other screens with sections of the roof collage. Something had penetrated his Cisco Firepower NGFW and selected one particular screen to taunt him.

The computer screen flicked back on, its image of the roof in high resolution. From the bed, ten feet away, Eddie could see the small figure. It hadn't moved from its perch on the roof. He waked back to the computer and sat down. Why not zoom in? He knew he should be pulling plugs and salvaging what he could, but the figure looked so small and insignificant, a little blob on the roof, almost a smudge in the greater scheme of his creation.

He zoomed. In almost crystal clarity, he could see long black braids decorated with yellow ribbons and sparkly bows descending down the back of the small head. Slowly the head turned at looked at him. It was that time jumper, that punk Nez Perce kid. Mazie, the brat, was sitting on the roof staring at him. She turned away and looked down at the parking lot. He zoomed again to see what was down there. Fuck, he was down there.

Trickster from hell, he screamed, yanking wires and pulling monitors away from the wall.

The parking lot was deserted. He drove his van up to the side entrance and stumbled inside, the rain pelting his back. Thank God he hadn't seen anyone standing in the parking lot. On the drive over he had convinced himself that it was just a Photoshop layer of an image of himself inserted onto the parking lot he had created, an invasion of his work, yes, but a simple visual deception. Nothing more, nothing less. But something about the way the image of himself looked concerned him. Too life-like, no tell-tale signs of animation. It could be a double, someone Mazie or her crazy NP family hired or coerced into dressing like him and playacting. Just in case it was a double, he had driven fast on a diagonal straight across the lot at high speed in order to run over anybody standing in that spot. He could always explain the impact away as an unintentional car accident. After all, he was the night janitor.

Next was the roof.

Dragging his leg, he hopped up the stairs and hobbled to the side where the brat had been sitting. No one. Walking the roof line, he didn't see any little girl leaning over any edge. Of course, what he had seen on his home computer could have been filmed earlier, but the night sky was exactly like it was tonight. How could the intruder simulate that? Weather reports perhaps and previous footage of storms in the area could be lifted, but not those leaves whirling under the lights on the south side next to the picnic tables. They were still swirling and skidding across the parking lot, stirring more dust into the already agitated air. Eddie's dry throat rattled and rasped as he tried to breathe. He was exhausted. He wanted to go to sleep. He collapsed at the roof's edge, making one last effort to think it through, when he noticed a car parked at the front of the church. He had been so eager to race through the parking lot and check out the roof that he hadn't even looked at the front of the church.

Sure enough, there was a car, and he couldn't see anyone sitting inside behind the steering wheel. Then he looked straight down and saw two people, one big, one small, huddled together on the front steps. From the shape of the head, one looked like a woman, the other was covered in something like a blanket.

Nobody fucks with me, Eddie thought. With a blast of energy drawn from the last reserves in his nervous system, he flung himself down the stairs, bolted out the back door and dragged himself across the side lawn to the front doorway.

:: FORTY-FOUR ::

The kid had an ally, an over-protective do-gooder who hated him at first glance. Maybe she was the person responsible for deleting a few thousands of his juicy comments on the dashcam, a genocide-averse snoop dog, an extermination blocker, fretting over words embedded in the heart. She looked the type— teary-eyed, earnest, and desperate for a reason to live, a typical educated, white woman with some sappy connection to the NP people. What was she doing with Mazie? After his tussle with the kid plus guardian on the steps and their fast getaway, he'd decided to let them escape. He had her license number and could find out what he needed through the Mormon computers. Jerry-rigging what he needed from the office machines to gain access to the Salt Lake mainframe, a programmer's dreamscape for locating the living and the dead, surveying souls, keeping people tuned into the Prophet's words, and searching for celestial and DNA evidence to enrich *THE SOURCE CODE OF CREATION*, he produced a social networking map of Larice's world. She had worked for twenty-three years at the local newspaper as a photojournalist, had three bad marriages, had recently reunited with an array of old high school friends found on Facebook, made a massive number of phone calls to the Nez Perce Tribal Headquarters, generating several interoffice emails that would take him more time to access, attended a grief therapy group at her sister's church, Mount Zion Baptist Rapture Central, and made several calls to Cass Zinski, the lawyer. Nothing about Mazie. There had to be a connection.

Hunched over the computer, Eddie sensed that his mind was functioning in ultraspeed, despite his periodic inability to move his head or lift his hands. His left leg felt like a stick that could snap into a dozen splinters if he swung it too hard or put much weight on it, not that he had much weight left. He must have lost thirty pounds over the last day and was dropping fast as each second ticked past. Ignoring his disabilities, he continued to hack away at the computer even when he kept having to recheck what he was doing twice, three times, sometimes five times, as he gathered data on Larice, his fingers trembling at the pace of his efforts, his mind constantly refocusing on the task at hand. Then, bingo, he found the big one. Larice had paid out over $3,000 to purchase a series of guaranteed curses on one single individual, the state cop who shot dead Mr. Hoop Dancer.

Then the pieces came together. An elaborate reconnect with old high school friends, the embarassing calls to the tribal receptionist, an amazing encounter, a blissful few days, then wham!!! Lover-boy shot dead, creating a wrecked woman who was duped into shelling out money online for gory revenge. What a loser. Eddie wished she knew how to shoot her gun. She should have come to him. He would have pointed her in the right direction with some tips on caliber and surprise. But someone like her could never have figured out he was the guy who put the cop's dashcam on YouTube, recreating her lover's death for millions of viewers every minute of every day, 24/7. All she wanted was the cop. Not him. Then how did she end up with Mazie? Coincidence? He doubted that. It must be the midget trickster up to a parallel game to the one she was playing with him online. Mazie wanted an analog time and space and had entrapped the poor old woman into playing along.

In the darkness Eddie wondered how Mazie would next attack. Probably send someone on a stealth mission. The thought produced the unshakeable feeling that someone was watching him as he was scrounging for data in the back office. He threw a cleaning rag over the eye and then hunted up some duct tape in the desk drawer and wrapped the top of the monitor. That little NP brat would try to get him to do something. Maybe she wanted him at the computer looking into Larice. That could be it. She drew him to the Mormon temple parking lot with her subterfuge visuals. After the pull-push with the woman and her ridiculous threats, she figured he would become obsessed with ruining the woman's life as well as the monster child's. Getting him to sit at the computer might be a diversion while another of the little trickster's allies was entering the building unnoticed. He quickly flicked on the lights and started searching with herculean effort every meeting room, prayer area, and bathroom. He decided not to go downstairs and check the basement because he didn't think his legs would get him back up the stairs. He could slide down, but not climb back, and his body was shaking from the effort he had already made.

What did Mazie want him to do next? He had to outsmart her. Maybe she had his look alike stashed somewhere in one of the closets. He hadn't checked the kitchen thoroughly and went back, rummaging in the cabinets, and looking through the refrigerator. Then he saw the half-way eaten banana cream pie in the garbage pail. Stuck to its gooey surface was a small bottle of Desert Essence and a paycheck stub from Subway. $273.48 paid to Al Zhang, the guy with the extra key.

Eddie routed around in the garbage bin and found inside a paper bag a stinky pair of rotting sandals; the stench made him want to puke from the mix of urine, dog poop, caked garbage, and petrol. The homeless guy. Mazie had left him a clue. The man with the rope had eaten pie with Subway Zhang and left with a good pair of shoes. She wanted him to find the man with the rope. But why?

He sat at the kitchen table and tried to think which was almost impossible since his eyes were starting to see only dark veils and strange pulsing lights, and simple things like the kitchen sink had started to look more like an enormous cavern with cascading waterfalls flowing over its edges.

After licking the banana cream filling from his itchy fingers, Eddie came to one conclusion. No such luck. He wouldn't play Mazie's game. He refused to chase the man with the rope or to search any further for ways to destroy Larice.

They can go to hell.

He wanted the girl, the mini-Lozen, the dwarf prophet, the tiny trickster, and he knew where to find her.

The van bumped onto the sidewalk and sped down the entire city block, crashing to a halt at Dave's Pawn Shop. The place was dark and buttoned tight. He yanked himself around the store, checking every window and door, pounding and yelling at the building. Nothing.

Parked close to the store was a white Volvo, packed with moving boxes and plastic bags filled with clothes and kitchen utensils. Getting a crowbar from the back of his van, he strode over and started smashing the windows. After the first few hits, he collapsed onto the dirt and let the bar slide from his hand. He couldn't stand to touch the metal. Too much pain. It was searing his hand. With a final effort, he grabbed the crowbar and spun with all his might, slamming the bar into the window. At last, the passenger window shattered into a sticky mass of fractured glass with a hand-size hole in the middle. He thrust his fingers through and opened the car door, stripping his hand of its last remaining skin. Shaking, he reached inside the glove compartment for the registration. He peered at the bloody piece of paper. *Al fuckin' Zhang.* The guy was like some kind of Asian plague, a plague sent from the trickster.

Eddie started to pull what was in the Volvo out onto the sidewalk and brown grass. He flung books, cans, plastic bottles, clothing, letters, photographs, and rolls of computer paper with perforated edges that he hadn't seen in at least twenty years. He didn't know what he was looking for, but he was convinced it was in the car. When he had everything out, he ran back to the store, turned around and started his frantic search again. He ran back and forth, again and again, repeating the same pattern: trash the car then bang on the store windows and doors.

He was going to get his gun out of his van and start shooting up the pawnshop when a woman emerged from the shadows and yelled at him to stop. In her right hand she had a gun aimed at his heart.

PART FIVE

MAGNETIC FIELDS

:: FORTY-FIVE ::

There is a stillness in a seed, a waiting to stir within its shiny surface, brittle and sharp, pillow-round, or moon-curved. Her eyes were not black but blackened from age and the grave. When the man with the rope held her in his hand, he wet his fingertip with his lips and gently touched the right eye first as if helping the doll into sight. The grime gave way to a golden seed stone the size of his little fingernail and he felt the curve of the hard eye come alive.

"Chokecherry." Dave took the doll from Sheldon and returned it to the large gun case sitting upright against the closet wall. "I thought they were dead girl's eyes, shriveled with hate. Only chokecherry seeds."

He looked as if he wanted to pluck them.

Sheldon stood in front of the doll's prison as if planning her escape. He turned to the owner, and the owner knew that Sheldon could see inside his emptiness. The doll's constant talking about the past had gutted him, stripped away his muscles and pulled out his tendons—not even his bones were solid, more like chewed sticks holding up a skin tent.

The doll was still talking, and if Sheldon couldn't hear her, he might as well leave. The owner wouldn't keep him anymore, hidden in the store.

"She will never stop," insisted Sheldon, thinking how Dave was foolish to hide the doll in the case as if that would protect him from the story or from the magnetic waves piercing earth.

"You have to take her out of her prison and bring her back to where she belongs." The man with the rope sat down on the dirty linoleum floor and started plucking at his clothes. His rope was wrapped around his right shoe, caked in soil and chunks of weeds, yellow star thistle, cheatgrass, and crupina. He gestured to Dave to sit down next to him. Groaning, the weight of his shoulders heavy with fatigue, the owner sat down in stages, his knees searching for stable ground.

"I know someone who will take her." He described to Dave how they would wrap her in a blanket and drive to the rez. Along the way, Thain would change into farmland and then the plateau, gulches, ravines, sage and wooded hills of the Clearwater Basin. How there would be shades of blue deepening to purple, how they would be breathless one minute and afraid to breathe the next, how they would pass homes with no doors and enter an exponential series of horizons, and how their trip would breach the barricade he had built around himself.

They sat and talked for quite a while listing hurts and untreatable wounds. After a long whining rant, the man with the rope grew impatient with Dave's complaint and his cruel need to blame. The owner didn't grasp that the magnetosphere granted no guarantees. Dave had to accept his thin sliver of life on the biofilm of earth, subject to a million casualties every nanosecond.

The doll only reminded. She did not condemn. He must return the doll. The drive would do him good.

After unlocking the case, Dave bundled the doll carefully in an old, red blanket, hoping to still her voice. He asked the man with the rope where they had to go next. Puzzled, the man suggested they wait since company was coming. On the other side of the wall, they heard arguing, shouting, stumbling, odd laughing, and what sounded like a basketball bouncing.

Dave raced to the electrical panel on the wall and pulled the lever. A metallic clang was followed by screams then silence.

"Now we get to see what we caught," whispered Dave as he uncovered a large mirror.

Peering through the one-way mirror, Sheldon was shocked to see a young girl in a peacock green dress looking straight at him, her gold-speckled brown eyes gleaming.

"Who the hell is that?" asked Dave.

"I don't know. Oh, wait a minute. I do."

It was the girl from McDonald's, but nobody in the room seemed to see her.

Three adults were huddled by a wall of Nez Perce cradle-boards; Al from Subway, Mrs. Holland from the dance studio, and Blake, the county cop that Sheldon had kept evading by hiding behind the dumpsters at the shopping mall parking lot. A few feet away, another woman was bent over, searching through a pile of documents on top of a stack of boxes. She didn't seem frightened at all, only earnest and snoopy. She was saying something to the trio and pointing to a tiny swaddled skeleton propped on a shelf. She kept repeating one word over and over that made Mrs. Holland clutch her forehead with both hands. Immediately, the cop started pacing the room looking for something he couldn't find.

"I know that woman poking around in my stuff," Dave said. "She works with the tribe. A woman lawyer. You know the type. Watch out for her. No good. What the fuck is she saying? One word over and over."

"Thief," said Sheldon.

"Fuck that," replied Dave. "That cop doesn't have jurisdiction here and he doesn't look like he could do a damn thing. What's he looking for? Is that the Chinese guy that works at Subway? What's he doing here and who the hell is that old lady?"

"That's Mrs. Holland from The Snake River Dance Studio and that other girl by the horse mask is her star student, Renee, the girl with green eyes. Oh, look, she noticed my little friend."

In a flash, the two girls were hugging and laughing, their questions falling like rain. Sheldon and Dave couldn't hear what was said, but after their reunion followed by information sharing and strategizing, Renee did the introductions while the adults shook their heads in disbelief and quickly formed a new huddle again about what the hell they were going to do now that two minors were involved.

Dave watched the pantomime until he couldn't stand it anymore. He spat on the floor then placed the blanket bundle down on an upended sea-green Frigidaire.

"We got a problem here." He went back to the gun case and hefted his MP5.

"Intruders."

The man with the rope stopped Dave and warned him that he could take his gun, but everyone had to join them, even the woman outside in the back of the store who had her own gun. If Dave followed directions, the stories in his head would go away. At least, he thought they would. The owner didn't have to worry about the woman with the gun, but she had to come. The man she wanted to shoot was minutes away from death and minutes away from a longer trip through the shadows that might take a few millenniums if the magnetosphere did not vaporize every living thing on earth by whim or accident before he died. It was not clear where shadowland would relocate when earth's GPS would obliterate. He laughed then because he had rhymed.

The lockdown bars were retracting into the ceiling when the man with the rope came out carrying a packet in his arms. Blake was not pleased at all to see the MP5 in Dave's hand when the door swung wide open.

"Put those down." The owner yelled at Cass who still had a bunch of papers clutched in her hand. "We're all going for a ride in my truck. You, there, you two kids, get behind me."

Ignoring him, Mazie skipped over to the man with the rope, her eyes bright beads lighting her way.

"Thank you, man with the rope."

Reaching to the blanket, she patted the bundle gently as if it were a child tossing in a sleepless night.

Once outside, Dave made the four adults climb in the back of his 1973 box truck and latched the door. The man with the rope and the two girls hopped inside the front. He walked around to the back of his store and found the woman Sheldon had described. She was looking down at what seemed a heap of clothes, her handgun dangling from the fingertips of her right hand. When she realized he was watching her, she dropped the gun and backed away.

"I didn't do a thing. Nothing."

"Maybe you did. Maybe you didn't. Doesn't matter. You're coming with me."

Once Larice was locked inside the back with Al, Cass, Blake, and Mrs. Holland, Dave lurched the truck onto Thain and headed toward Cottonwood Creek on the rez.

"Can you smell the river?" asked Sheldon.

Mazie had the red bundle on her lap and was slowly unwrapping the blanket.

"Don't touch that," shouted Dave.

"No worry," said Sheldon. "It's hers."

Mazie lifted the doll from the blanket and set it on her lap. The one golden eye and the one black eye stared back at her. She handed it to Renee who tried to look under the cornhusk skirt. "It's a little stinky," she said.

"Not enough air. Not enough dirt. Not enough water."

They drove for about twenty minutes out of town, then bumped along a gravel road for a few miles. Mazie looked out the window and caught a glimpse of the Clearwater.

"There," she pointed. "Right there."

Sheldon grabbed the steering wheel and turned the truck hard, almost flipping it on its side and sending the back passengers into a screaming fit.

"Brake now," Mazie yelled.

She jumped down from the truck and asked Renee to hand her the doll. Renee left the blanket inside and followed Mazie to the riverbed. Together they stooped down, their shoes touching the cold, swift water, and released the doll, scooting her into the current that twisted the doll for a second, washing her head and body, then sending her floating fast downstream. The man with the rope and Dave had climbed out and together they watched the doll bob and turn until a large boulder swept her around its whitewater foam and out of sight.

Returning, they could hear banging and kicking from the back of the truck.

"Now what?" Dave asked the man with the rope. "Should I set them loose? They will be as mad as hell."

"One more stop, then we let them go."

For twenty miles, the truck sped east on Highway 12 until it swerved onto a graded county road, raced past every stop sign, took a hard right, crashed over a gravel berm and wound its way down a rutted road to a narrower dirt road, then up a long hill that wound around a cluster of rusting cars until it stopped in front of a double wide trailer.

Dave opened the back of the truck and five disheveled souls, pissed and swearing, fell out, dazed.

"Kidnapper," shouted Mrs. Holland at Dave. "And you, homeless fiend."

She plunged at the man with the rope but was held back by Blake while Al shoved in Dave's face the Chinese character for *listen* that he had written on his palm. Bedlam. Amid threats about lost wages and mathematical anomalies, Cass, still clutching the papers she had never let go, grabbed the man with the rope, stomped up to the double wide, and banged loud until William wearing sweats and a star-covered vest opened the door.

Not at all surprised, he motioned for the man with the rope to come inside and shouted at Dave to follow. "You too," he added, welcoming the girls.

Dave set his MP5 down next to the truck and walked up the incline to the front steps. He knew where he was and what he had to do.

"Everybody else stay outside!" ordered William, slamming the door in Cass's face.

Inside the house his wife, Lydia, brewed mountain tea. Dave handed the Ellyns his meticulously itemized inventory with the keys to his pawnshop. They thanked him and shook his hand, telling him freedom could not be bought, but it was a good step in the right direction. Feeling flutters of sadness, Dave joined the girls on the couch.

What then happened in the Ellyn's living room led to wild speculations in the town and on the reservation. The man with the rope described the police officer's face and explained how his whirling rage upset the magnetosphere, twisting lines into permanent knots that unbalanced Sheldon's fragile equilibrium. Worse, the hate face seized the police officer, plunging him into a spacetime bulge. After all, the state trooper's face was made by thousands of carvers applying patinas of hate, fear, and self-loathing over centuries. Bang, bang, bang, bang, bang, his gun blasted wide wound channels, exerting hydrostatic pressures inside VE's body liquids. Hate expands and penetrates.

Comparing notes about eye-witness testimony, Renee and William deliberated whether to pursue legal counsel while Mazie snuck out the front door. Unaware of this escape, Lydia asked Sheldon if he wanted to stay for a few months and help her with the coming camas harvest and the new science curriculum at the middle school.

Initial plans concluded, William invited everyone inside. Larice ignored the offer to share a meal and eat the leftover Krispy Kremes from a Defusing Anger in the Workplace meeting on the reservation. Like a scent hound, she walked up and down the rutted dirt road. She was back. She was where the hoop dancer, her beloved, was shot dead. She wandered behind the trailer and headed down the hill, stopping at the tree stump where the cop had collapsed after shooting VE five times. She kept going down to the clump of chokecherry trees where her lover died, not right away, but after twelve minutes of blood running from his heart and arms, down his legs and into the earth.

"Blood spiller," she hissed. Then she touched the leaves of the tree shifting in the wind. "Dancer," she said. "Bold dancer."

Mazie found Larice still as a statue and curled her fingers round the woman's hand, their warmth stirring her heart. Next came Renee, fearless in the dark, who never doubted the excruciating power of grief.

After a while, the man with the rope slowly made his way down to the trees. Despite the recent legal advice on his rights, he still counted on the corn doll drifting to keep the world safe. As magnetic lines snapped through the sky, fraying threads loosened their hold around his waist. Step by step, he steadied himself as he stumbled to find the girls and the strange woman with tears in her eyes.

Silence enveloped the night, music sounding through stars. Clustered together, they listened while the wind played tricks and the smell of river rose to greet them.

ABOUT THE AUTHOR

For more than thirty years, Joan Burbick lived in the Palouse region of northern Idaho and eastern Washington writing and teaching at Washington State University with periodic stints as a visiting professor at universities in Beijing, Hong Kong, and Warsaw. At present, she resides on an island off the coast of Washington. Her two nonfiction books, *Rodeo Queens and the American Dream* and *Gun Show Nation: Gun Culture and American Democracy* were based on years of interviewing people about how the myths of the West shape everyday life. These interviews led her to many people whose lives were dramatically altered by violence. And their stories led her to *Stripland*, her first novel.

redbat
books

For other titles available from redbat books, please visit:
www.redbatbooks.com

Also available through Ingram, Amazon.com,
Barnesandnoble.com, Powells.com and by special order
through your local bookstore.

CPSIA information can be obtained
at www.ICGtesting.com
Printed in the USA
FFHW020911100519
52390579-57798FF